The Duke's Unexpected Courtship

Georgia Griffan

Table of Contents

Prologue

Chapter 1: A Start to the Season

Chapter 2: Dressed to Impress

Chapter 3: A Debut

Chapter 4: An Obligation to Dance

Chapter 5: A Morning in London

Chapter 6: What Happens at Night

Chapter 7: A Woman's Honour

Chapter 8: A Bride & Groom

Chapter 9: Breakfast

Chapter 10: The Dowager Duchess' Picnic

Chapter 11: What Happens in the Library

Chapter 12: The Beulle Ball

Chapter 13: Afterwards

Chapter 14: The Aberlay Ball

Chapter 15: A Denouement

Chapter 16: What Honour Demands

Chapter 17: Wedding Jitters

Chapter 18: In Sickness and in Health

Chapter 19: Honeymoon Days

Chapter 20: London Again

Chapter 21: The Duke and Duchess

Prologue

Kit's father, the Duke of Aberlay, was by many accounts the richest man in England. The majority of his vast holdings stretched across the flat agricultural lands of the midlands, generating so much income in produce and rent a dozen clerks and an army of secretaries were required to administer it. Then there was the highland estate where the Duke went hunting in summer, the orchards in Kent that sent up apples for his table every autumn without fail, the rows of townhouses and commercial buildings in London and Bath, the interests in shipping, the Welsh mines and innumerable other possessions generating revenue and income that the Duke hardly troubled himself to know about.

With so many matters to occupy his time, it was no wonder the Duke had little time for his only son and heir. Kit, or the Marquess of Kittrington to use his proper title, had been born precisely eighteen years ago to a relieved Duke and Duchess. Seven long years of marriage had resulted in a series of miscarriages and a single daughter who could not inherit. When at last the longed for son arrived, it was said the Duke was so happy he'd pronounced the newborn perfect and kissed him three times, an unusual display of affection for the taciturn Duke.

This incident was reported to the young boy so many times, that despite only seeing his father on a handful of occasions, he was left in no doubt as to the man's affection. And besides, few men of his father's station paid much attention to their children growing up. Kit had every expectation that adulthood would bring a closer relationship with the Duke. He imagined his father, at last, taking him into his confidence, sharing with Kit the workings of his estates, how such a large enterprise was managed. Perhaps they would hunt together now that Kit was at university and nearly a man himself.

His father might pat him on the back after a particularly good shot or casually impart some advice while stalking deer. He had often written to his father seeking the closer relationship he wanted, but the Duke seldom replied and when he did it was with a few hastily written lines. No matter, the man was busy. Kit knew that. It was why he'd left Oxford for a few days to travel to London. If he wanted to spend time with the Duke, it made sense for Kit to go to him rather than asking his father to take time out of a busy schedule.

As the carriage rolled to a stop outside the Duke of Aberlay's massive townhouse, trepidation and excitement rolled through Kit in equal measure. He had never spent time with just his father. Although he was confident of the Duke's love, he also wanted the man to like and respect him. Kit hoped that through study and application, he was shaping into a person worthy of his father's admiration and a suitable heir for the Dukedom.

"Lord Kittrington. You are not expected," said the footman opening the door with a frown.

"I sent a letter ahead, but perhaps I have preceded it. No matter," said Kit, "There is no need for any great preparations. I am only here to see my father after all."

"My Lord, I am not sure this is a good time," said the footman, trying to shut the door, "His Grace is indisposed."

"Then I must go to him at once," cried Kit barging past. "If my father is in ill health he will be all the more glad to see me."

"No, My Lord, please wait -" insisted the footman. But Kit didn't listen, bounding up the stairs in great strides.

Grand double doors stood at the end of the corridor, the entrance to the master bedroom. Muffled sounds came from within. Kit frowned, his hand turning the doorknob. Was his father crying out in pain?

The door swung open and Kit recoiled in horror. His father wasn't in pain. Quite the opposite. A naked woman bounced vigorously up and down atop his father, the curls atop her head and her ample breasts swinging in time to her rhythm. The Duke was just as naked, but mercifully his position, beneath her, meant that Kit could see less of him.

"Oh God," cried Kit.

"Oh God," cried the woman.

Kit slammed the door shut, but not before Kit caught his father's gaze.

When Kit next saw his father, he was dressed, albeit in little more than a robe. Even in that, the Duke managed to look aloof and intimidating. It didn't help that he was visibly furious. Kit wilted under his father's glare.

"What are you doing here?"

"I came to see you," said Kit.

"Why would you think I would want to see you? Have I ever given any indication that I did?" spat the Duke.

Hurt blossomed in Kit's chest and quickly turned to anger. "Of course not. It is clearly too much to hope that a father would want to spend time with his son rather than a whore who instead of meeting secretly, he brings to the Ducal townhouse, flaunting his betrayal of my mother before all the servants."

"How dare you reprimand me. Do you think for a moment your mother even cares? Go to her now and tell her. I assure you she won't. She has everything she ever wanted. A generous allowance and the title of Duchess before her name. And I have fulfilled my duty as far as a wife and heir are concerned."

This wounded Kit deeply. "Is that all your family is to you? A duty that needs to be fulfilled. Do you care so little for us?"

The Duke scoffed. "You stupid, naive boy. Dukes don't marry for affection. They don't have families for love. If they did, I would've married my mistress. But the dignity of my position required marriage to a lady. Your mother was happy to accept this given the nature of the prize."

"Sleeping too long in the gutter has sullied your mind. The woman in your bed might be driven there by money, but do not project her failings onto mother."

"Whether the price is matrimony or coin, the instinct behind it is the same. All women look to a man's wealth before deciding whether he is worthy of her bed. Your wife will be no different. And when she gives you a son, you will also look at that child as a fulfilment of your duty to the Ducal title."

Kit blinked away the moisture in his eyes. He was almost a man and men did not cry, not even on hearing their fathers held no love for them, that he was only a necessary duty. "I am not you. I will not marry so cynically and without affection."

The Duke laughed. A cruel sound. "How will you know? You think the lady you seek to marry will not behave as if she truly loves you? But inside will be the cold calculation of her gender, the knowledge that you are to inherit a Dukedom and one of the greatest fortunes in England. And that knowledge will cloud any romance. Disabuse yourself of that notion now and you shall avoid a bitter heartbreak in the future."

"Like I should disabuse myself of my father's love?"

"Love is for children and fools, and no Aberlay is a fool," said the Duke.

It was Kit's last conversation with his father. The next day he left for the continent to join the British army in its great fight against Napoleon. If he died in battle, and deprived the Duke of his heir, well that would be a fitting retribution. Now it was his father's turn to send frantic letters, urging his only son to give up this mad enterprise and return to England. Kit took great delight in ignoring him.

Chapter 1
A Start to the Season

1812

7 years later

Breakfast was a tense affair at the Duefont's London Townhouse. A frown line had developed between Lady Duefont's brow almost as soon as they'd arrived in London and it grew deeper each day. From what Ada could tell, the only person unaffected by the approaching season was their father, Sir Walter Duefont. He sat as calmly as ever, reading his paper, completely oblivious to the feelings of the ladies surrounding him.

Beside Ada, her older sister Henrietta practically buzzed with excitement. With a glittering London season already behind her, the last few months of country balls must have seemed unbearably dull to Hetty. But Ada had no such comparison to make. She had only just come out, and this was her first London season. The balls back in Riverstoke village had seemed grand enough to her, and the thought of attending one of the great balls of London made her exceedingly nervous.

Lady Duefont could no longer contain herself. "Where can that blasted woman be? Madame Jacqueline promised the dress would be delivered yesterday! And now it's the morning of the season's opening ball and Henrietta has nothing to wear!"

At the outburst, Sir Walter peered over the top of his paper to look at his wife in some astonishment. "What on earth do you mean my dear lady? Henrietta has dozens of gowns, any one of which is perfectly suitable attire."

"An older gown might suffice for Ada, who is never going to be much of a beauty anyway, but Henrietta must have the latest fashion to show her off to the best. She has a real chance of making a very excellent match, and we can't ruin it for her with shabby out-of-fashion gowns."

Ada tried to ignore the throwaway comment about her looks. She knew she was no beauty, especially in comparison to Henrietta with her golden locks and delicate features. Mother was just stating the facts. If one of them was to make an advantageous match it would be Hetty. She was beautiful enough to catch the eye of some of the tons most eligible bachelors, and once besotted they might not mind so much that their father was only a baronet.

"Oh mother," burst in Hetty, "don't be such a bore. It's Ada's first season. She should be shown to form."

Their mother sniffed, "Of course I have ordered a new gown for Ada too. But you know what I mean. Why Hetty, the Duke could offer for you this season! Just imagine it, my daughter, the Duchess of Aberlay."

With less than thirty Dukes in the whole of the British Isles, and only one of them unwed and of age, the Duke of Aberlay was far and away the most coveted prize in the marriage mart. Every matron, mother and debutant was manoeuvring to snare him. But from what the gossip papers wrote, he was far too cold and proud to make a match inferior to his lofty position. And by her father's incredulous snort, she wasn't the only one who thought so.

"You might as well imagine Hetty marrying the prince regent! The Aberlays are the most connected family in the ton, the whole lot of them are snobs. We should have accepted any one of the perfectly suitable gentlemen who asked for Hetty's hand last season. Instead your ridiculous manoeuvring will lead nowhere except poor Hetty remaining a spinster. At least you will not be so silly Ada, you'll be happy with a reasonable proposal."

"Well, of course, any gentleman of means will do for Ada," said their mother, "But I won't have you spoiling Hetty's chances with your pessimism. A woman's station in life depends on the marriage she makes." The last sentence was said with a pointed look in Sir Walter's direction.

Ada winced, bracing herself for the inevitable argument. Her mother had, in her view, married beneath herself. As the daughter of a Baron, she had hoped to marry a peerage. And it didn't help that her sisters had managed it, with one a Countess and the other a Baroness through their marriages. Her mother, having not the beauty of her sisters, nor a personality that might have made up for it, had to settle for the best suite she'd been offered, which happened to be Sir Walter. It was an old resentment that flared up periodically.

Sir Walter, as a mere baronet, was not a member of the peerage and marriage to him meant that their mother was now of a lower rank than both her own mother and her sisters. It was a state of affairs that made their mother anxious that one of her daughters (Henrietta) should at least regain the position she had lost.

By his red face and furrowed brows, Ada could see that their father was preparing himself for a sharp rebuke. She wondered if her father regretted his choice of wife. Though not as prestigious, he might have been happier married to a woman of the lesser gentry, who would not feel she had been demeaned by marriage to him.

There was a sharp knock on the front door and Ada used the opportunity to avert an argument. Before her father could speak she burst out, "That must be Madam Jacquline with the dresses! Who else would call at this hour before the season has even begun?"

Lady Duefont all but leapt out of her chair and into the hallway, not even waiting for the butler to announce their guest as was proper. The sound of raised voices carried through into the breakfast room and then their mother's head popped through the entryway.

"Girls come quickly, Madame Jacquline is here at last."

Hetty and Ada hurried into the drawing room where an assistant was carefully placing the dress boxes on a table.

"Lady Duefont, I am so sorry," Madame Jacquline was saying as she carefully unwrapped the gowns, "You zee, it was the Duchess. A last minute alteration. And one does not refuse a summons from Her Grace, not if one wishes to continue doing business in London."

Her mother's face turned speculative, "The Dowager Duchess of Aberlay? But Almacks is a week away and she normally doesn't attend the opening balls. Why would she need a dress altered so urgently?"

Madame Jacquline hesitated, reluctant to reveal the personal business of her clients.

"You know the dresses arriving late has caused us such a great deal of panic, Madame Jacquline. And I know many of my friends in the ton, and indeed my own sisters, highly value punctuality in a dressmaker."

The threat worked. "I only know what ze servants say. It seems His Grace, ze Duke of Aberlay, is seriously considering taking a wife. If not zis season, then ze next. And his mother, she is determined to help him. She threw a small soiree last night, before ze official start of season, with many young, eligible women there."

"Interesting," said their mother. Ada could almost see the cogs turning in her brain as she processed this new information. Perhaps it would make Mama see how unlikely the idea of Hetty marrying the Duke was. They hadn't even been considered by the Dowager Duchess. If Mama would lower her ambitions slightly, Hetty might land a Viscount or even an Earl, which in itself would be an incredible match.

"Perhaps, Lady Duefont, you'll forgive my lateness given the circumstances?" asked Madame Jacquline.

"Of course, of course," said their mother with a magnanimous wave, "After all the dresses are here and I am sure they are lovely."

Her business reputation secured, Madame Jacquline removed the last layer of protective wrapping over the dresses.

Ada gasped at just how lovely they were. Hetty's was the most eye-catching of course. Done in a rich, bright fabric and designed to grab attention. But she liked hers better. It was simpler and perhaps not so much the latest fashion, but it was beautiful.

"Put them on girls, quickly," said their mother.

Ada rushed to obey, shimmying out of her comparatively plain day dress and stepping into the shimmering white silk. Mama was busy cooing over the brocade on Henrietta's dress, which left Ada mercifully in peace to savour the feel of the sumptuous fabric on her skin.

"Let me help you, ma cherie," said Madame Jacquline, realising that between their mother and the assistant, Henrietta had more than enough hands.

Ada gave her a grateful smile. She was used to being overlooked for Hetty, but it was quite impossible to get this gown to fasten properly without assistance.

"Your mama was very specific about your sister's dress. But I had quite a bit of artistic freedom with yours and I think ze results are better for it," said Madame Jacquline quietly as she did up the tiny pearl buttons that went the length of the bodice.

"It is a beautiful gown," said Ada.

Madam Jacquline nodded. "Sometimes simple is more eye-catching. A lot of ze girls, they use feathers and jewels and loud colours to catch attention. Compared to them, you will look fresh and uncluttered. Zis dress, it is beautiful, bien sur, but more importantly, it shows off *your* beauty."

"It is kind of you to say so, but I am no beauty."

Madame Jacquline's eyebrows rose in surprise. "You really mean that. There is no false modesty in your voice. You have, as we say en France, a certain je ne sais quoi. There is a sensuality combined with innocence that men will find irresistible. It would not surprise me if you were proclaimed zis season's *incomparable*."

And with that astonishing statement, Madame Jacquline went to adjust some folds on Henrietta's dress. Adeline chuckled slightly to herself. The season's incomparable indeed! Too much late-night stitching had clearly ruined Madame Jacquline's eyesight, that or her mind was addled. But the thought of someone finding her lovely, even if it was just an old seamstress with terrible eyesight filled her with a warm glow.

Eventually, achieving sufficient satisfaction with Henrietta's outfit, her mother walked over. "You look very pretty, darling."

It was kindly said and Adeline responded with a smile. "Thank you, Mama. Hopefully it will help me find a match this season."

Mama nodded, her gaze drifting towards Hetty's direction.

"It is a shame you got my darker looks. Both my sisters had golden hair just like Henrietta and it served them well in the marriage-mart. I think if you'd inherited the lighter-looks in our family, you would've been just as beautiful as Henrietta, after all, there is nothing glaringly wrong with your face and figure."

And with that casual remark her mother burst the warm glow left from Madame Jacquline's words. Ada swallowed hard against the sudden thickness in her throat. Despite her common-sense telling her otherwise, for a second maybe a small part of her had believed in what Madame Jacquline said. That she wasn't the ugly sister, but rather a woman with beauty and attractiveness of her own. Mama had quickly disabused her of that notion.

Unaware of the emotional turmoil she'd caused in her youngest daughter, Lady Duefont clapped her hands together, the sharp sound bringing everyone to attention. "The dresses will do wonderfully, and now the girls must be getting ready. It is already midday."

Ada looked towards the mantlepiece clock with some alarm. In fact it was a little past midday. Trying on the dresses and making the small alterations that were always needed had taken the better part of an hour. A few more hours like this and she would be at her first ever London ball. A nervous shiver went down her spine and she felt the prickle of goosebumps on her skin.

Some of their maids had come down to take the dresses and steam them for tonight. Ada carefully slipped the white silk dress off and handed it over. Putting her cotton day-dress back on afterwards felt like a disappointment. In comparison it was coarse and inelegant. Ada shook her head ruefully at herself. She was no Princess or Duchess to be always adorned in velvet and silks. A well-made cotton dress would do just fine for her. And besides, tonight at the ball she would feel nothing but silk on her skin for hours. If only the experience didn't come with a huge side-dose of trepidation.

"Into the bath with both of you! And get their hair into papers!" barked out their mother, "We're already behind schedule!"

Chapter 2
Dressed to Impress

In the end, Ada was hardly in her cotton dress for any time at all. Upon reaching her bedchambers, the dress along with all her undergarments, stays and stockings were efficiently stripped off by her mother's maid, Marie and her own maid, Blanche.

A claw-footed tub at the base of her bed had been filled with steaming-hot water, and Ada was ushered, rather insistently into it to soak. Across the room, her sister's maid, Sarah, had already deposited Hetty into an identical tub and was busy putting away the day clothes.

"I'll be back in twenty minutes," said Marie leaving with a degree of haste, the door slamming behind her.

Although it was really Blanche's job to get Ada ready, considering the importance of the occasion, her mother had instructed her own, more experienced lady's maid to oversee the proceedings. Understandably, Marie was rushed off her feet, having to get both her own lady ready and make sure Blanche did a good job tonight. Adeline hadn't thought about it, but it was Blanche's first London ball too, and perhaps the young woman also felt the same nervousness that sat low in Ada's belly.

"Alright, Blanche?"

Her maid nodded, "I've been practising with Marie and Sarah. How to do the more elaborate hairstyles and apply the lotions. Besides, they'll help me the first time. It will be fine, you'll look lovely Miss Adeline."

"I don't doubt it," she said with a smile.

"What are you two nattering about?" called out Hetty in that clear, confident tone she had.

"I was just thinking that it was both mine and Blanche's first ball. But she is a lot less nervous than I am," said Ada with a small self-conscious laugh.

"You've no reason to be nervous, you'll do wonderfully Ada, I just know it. Besides, you've been training for this practically your whole life. Nothing will go wrong. It will all be incredibly dull and uneventful and at the end you'll think, is that what I was so worried about?"

"Was your first ball of the season like that? Dull and uneventful?"

"Oh, yes," said Hetty, "No one important or interesting ever turns up to the first ball, only the debutantes who need to be presented. And perhaps a few gentlemen hunting for fortunes, since they can scope out the market before the general ton, so to speak."

"But the Queen will be there! Surely that is enough to make any ball eventful," said Ada.

Hetty gave a noncommittal shrug that sent the water in her tub splashing slightly around her. "Queen Charlotte is old and uninterested in society. She will give her nod to each debutant and that will be it. Then there will be some dancing, where most of the ladies will not dance for want of male partners, followed by a cold supper and a carriage ride home. The whole thing is a bore. You'll be thoroughly underwhelmed," promised Hetty.

Their bedchamber door burst open and Marie came through, followed by a veritable army of housemaids. Another, smaller tub was placed in the middle of the room and bucket after bucket of water emptied into it.

"Good grief! Have we hired all the housemaids in London? What on earth is going on?" exclaimed Ada.

Hetty laughed at her confusion and unabashedly naked, stood up and out of her tub. "I'll go first," and made to get into the fresh tub of water.

"We've already bathed," said Ada in confusion.

"First a hot soak then a quick cold dip to polish the skin," said Marie as a way of explanation.

Hetty yelped as her skin hit the water and her body shivered hard, "I always forget how awful this is. The things we do for beauty," she managed to get out, her teeth chattering. In another second she was out and quickly wrapped in a warm blanket by her maid, Sarah.

"Your turn, Miss Adeline," said Marie.

Most of the maids had cleared out which made her less self-conscious of her lack of clothing. She got up, dashed across the room and slipped into the new tub. "It's freezing!" she cried out, shocked at the icy coldness seeping through her body. A feeling like pins and needles spread across her skin.

"Out you get, wouldn't do to catch a cold," instructed Marie going by some sort of internal clock.

Adeline hastened to obey, leaving with a tremendous splash, grateful to be out of that engulfing iciness. Blanche wrapped a warm blanket around her and in minutes Ada began to feel warm and dry again.

Blanche carefully trimmed Ada's nails and smoothed a scented balm over her skin to soften it. Lotions were applied all over her body, from her forehead all the way to her toes and then Blanche powdered her skin with a light dusting and applied perfume and finally a bit of rouge. While Blanche worked on her body, Marie did her hair, wrapping the locks into tight curls and setting it with papers.

"There, that's the initial preparations done," said Marie with satisfaction, "get the underclothes ready while I see to Lady Deufont."

"The initial preparations?" said Ada faintly, "This is already more than we ever did for a Riverstoke ball!"

"This is London, Ada. Riverstoke didn't matter because there weren't any men of consequence there," said Hetty, choosing between different pairs of stockings. She rolled one up her leg and deciding it was too sheer, took it off and tossed the rejected pair at Sarah to put away.

"I can't help thinking this is all slightly ridiculous. It's not going to change what I look like." said Ada.

"Wait until you see yourself after they're done. You'll swallow your words," promised her sister.

On went the chemise, the stockings picked out for her, the corset and finally the beautiful, luminescent gown. Just feeling it on her skin again made Ada feel a hundred times more elegant. Next to her Hetty had also slipped on her gown and Ada's heart sank a little, even as she admired her sister's beauty.

Next to Hetty, no man was likely to pay her much attention. The evening's preparations had made her sister even lovelier. Henrietta's skin positively glowed, her eyes looked brighter and her cheeks rosier, no doubt with the help of some rouge. All her life, Ada had been used to being the ugly duckling in comparison to Hetty's swan. But it had never really mattered until now.

Although she would never marry as well as Hetty, Ada did want to have a husband and a family of her own. Her dreams were modest, an untitled gentleman who was kind and not too old, who she loved or could come to love in time. Even if he was not particularly wealthy, they could live modestly on her dowry. There would be no seasons in London or fancy dresses or jewels but perhaps a small country house somewhere and a quiet village life raising her children. It was not glamorous, but Ada could be happy with that.

Last season, Hetty had received five proposals. At mother's insistence, their father had turned them all down. Most had been gentlemen equal in station and means to their father, including a couple of baronets and a third son of an Earl. But mother was determined that nothing less than a peerage would do for Henrietta, convinced that her oldest daughter's beauty was enough to snare even a Duke. Luckily, she wasn't so particular when it came to Ada. Mother would be happy to accept the hand of any gentleman for her younger daughter. If just one man would propose to her this year, she would be content, thought Ada.

The door slammed open, bringing not just Marie, but their mother bustling through as well. Mother looked elegant and suitably dressed for a woman of her station, although less elaborately outfitted than her daughters, her dark, plum-coloured gown was still far nicer than anything Ada had seen her mother wear before.

"I have brought jewels for you to wear tonight my girls," said Mama. And in her arms were nestled a stack of expensive looking velvet boxes. "A set of pearls for you Ada, and for my darling Hetty, my best sapphire necklace to bring out your eyes."

Peering inside the box offered to her, Ada saw the most perfect necklace of creamy pearls, each one a good size with few irregularities. There were matching drop earrings and a number of hairpins with pearl heads.

"How exquisite," said Ada. Though not as expensive as the sapphires currently being placed on Hetty's neck, she would be quite satisfied to wear these.

Ada glanced over at her sister. Hetty's eyes, lighter than her own, were not quite the same colour as the sapphires she wore but the effect was still enthralling, somehow the jewels made her sister's eyes sparkle, while drawing attention to their colouring.

Hetty caught Ada looking and in a sudden burst of kindness said, "Oh mama, why not let Ada wear the sapphires tonight. After all it is her debutante ball."

"There will be suitors there tonight," exclaimed Mama, "We know the Duke of Aberlay is looking for a bride and there might be other men of the peerage attending as well."

"Pfft. Hardly any high-ranking gentlemen come to the debutante ball. It is too tedious an affair for them to bother with. And the Duke is hardly going to subject himself to it. He could go to any ball of the season and pick any woman to be his bride. Tonight's ball will be full of second sons who need to woo wives with handsome dowries."

"I suppose you're right. The Queen's ball seldom brings out the best of the ton's gentlemen," conceded Mama, "Very well, Ada may wear the sapphires, but only tonight."

The switch was made immediately by their efficient maids and Ada looked down to see glittering sapphires instead of pearls. She felt Blanche fasten the sapphire jewels to her ears and slip on a bracelet encrusted with rich stones that felt cold against her skin. This set of jewellery was heavier than the pearls, and the weight of them caused Ada to hold her head up a little higher and her back a little straighter.

"The papers should be about ready to come out, Miss Ada," said Blanche, glancing at Marie who gave a nod of agreement.

"Do it carefully," instructed Mama, "the last thing we want is for everyone to say Ada has flat hair."

Slipping the papers gently off each of Ada's curls proved to be the most laborious task of the entire evening. It didn't help that Mama, now completely ready herself, interjected with her own instructions periodically. "No, do the bottom curl first, and don't pull it out straight."

Ada could feel Blanche's hands shaking slightly as nerves got the better of her.

"Don't worry Blanche, no one will notice if my curls are flat with this great, glittering necklace on my chest," said Ada quietly so only her maid could hear.

Blanche giggled and from then on her hands were surer and more steady. The last of the papers slid off with ease and her maid stepped back with a smile of satisfaction on her face. "You look beautiful Miss Ada. Why you'll be the loveliest debutante there."

Ada didn't believe it. She had always been called plain, but when she went to look in the glass she could see that Blanche had not been entirely false.

Although Ada would never be called beautiful, the preparations had at least made her seem elegant, and the overall look was pleasing. Reflected in the mirror was a great lady, clad in high fashion and adorned in glittering gems. The sapphires, slightly too dark for Hetty's eyes, matched perfectly with the deeper shades of Ada's, making her own eyes almost look like glittering jewels themselves. And whatever lotions and creams they'd applied to her skin had certainly done something. Her face looked creamier and softer, her complexion slightly flushed from the subtle application of rouge.

She'd never be a diamond of the first water, but for the first time Ada felt confident that some man would find her handsome enough to dance with at least. And then she could talk with him and hopefully he would find her company pleasant enough to think of making her his wife. Ada began to fix the image of such a man in her mind. He'd be ignored by most of the richer and well-connected marriageable women because of his lack of title and fortune. Perhaps he'd have a crumbling country estate somewhere that would generate just enough income for a modest life, supported by Ada's dowry. He might even be nice to look at if she was very lucky. Not devastatingly handsome of course, because such a man would garner a lot of interest from heiresses wealthier than Ada, but a quiet sort of good looks that weren't attention grabbing but grew on you with time. Yes, such a man would suit her perfectly indeed.

"Ready on time, this is already markedly better than our last debutante ball!" said mother, looking at her pocket watch, "Downstairs now both of you."

It was a source of great pride to Sir Walter that he was able to keep his own carriage and horses in London, and he was engaged in animated conversation with the coachman when the ladies finally bustled through the front door. A couple of Cleveland Bays, chestnut-brown in colour and similar in height and age stood proudly at the front, heads held high, as if they knew they were the subject of the men's conversation.

"Oh aye, Sir, they're in good spirits, to be sure! Not tired after the trip down to London at all," said the coachman.

"Breeding always shows in these things. The quality of the horseflesh was clear from the moment I saw them," said Sir Walter.

"Right ye are, Sir! They're fine specimens to be sure."

"It's a shame we cannot keep four horses like my sisters," said Mama, eyeing the pair of bays critically.

Their father visibly deflated, and the coachman hurried to clamber onto his seat, suddenly deaf to the conversation of his employers.

"We are lucky enough to have two horses to pull our carriage, lady wife, and a fine pair at that. Many families are not so fortunate," said Sir Walter, a tone of reprimand creeping into his voice.

Lady Duefont arched an eyebrow. "Luck has nothing to do with it. Unless you count it as luck to have a wife with a large enough dowry to maintain her family's coach in London."

Her father's face reddened and he climbed in to the carriage without a word, leaving the ladies to ascend as best they could. Ada sighed. They were in for a tense journey. In her less charitable moments, Ada found it unsurprising that her mother had had so few suitors for her hand. The difference in her parent's station meant that Sir Walter was dependent on his wife's fortune to maintain their family's lifestyle. It was a source of embarrassment for him that he had bought comparatively little to the marriage other than an indebted estate and good breeding, a fact which Mama seldom let him forget. Perhaps if her mother showed more consideration for others, she might have made a better match.

Although Ada was no handsomer than her mother, at least she could try and make up for it with kindness and good humour. If she were to find herself dancing with a suitable gentleman, she would make sure to be polite and well-mannered. At least her personality might endear her to potential suitors, even though her looks would not.

"Adeline, get in!" came her mother's shrill voice.

With the skirts of three ladies to accommodate, the inside of the carriage was if not exactly cramped, then certainly cosy. Ada carefully arranged the fabric of her silk dress so that it wouldn't be crushed and sat down as lightly as possible to avoid creasing the back. Her father tapped his cane against the panelled wall and off they went. A tense silence descended among the four passengers, broken only by the sounds of the wheels hitting the cobbled streets.

Ada turned to stare out the window. The remnants of the setting sun were turning the sky pink and bathing the white, Georgian townhouses of Mayfair in a golden glow. As they passed the wide, tree-lined streets, a carriage crossed their path and Ada spotted a finely dressed lady inside, engaged in animated conversation with whoever sat opposite. Probably her husband, thought Ada with a smile, they might be newlyweds off to a night at the opera. Ada craned her neck to see better.

"Ada, stop gawking through the window. Someone might see you, and think you a complete bumpkin," said Mama sharply.

Ada sat back abruptly. She had no desire to be the subject of her mother's ire. Ada knew first hand how biting Lady Duefont could be when provoked and Mama's casual sharp-tongued barbs were bad enough without being specifically directed towards Ada. As the carriage continued down the streets of London, and dusk turned to complete darkness, Ada satisfied herself with small darting glances at the blurred landscape going past.

Chapter 3
A Debut

Although by no means late, neither were they early if the number of carriages crowding outside St James's palace was any indication. The Deufont's coachman joined the end of the long queue of vehicles making incremental progress towards the gate. Ada had seen the grand stately homes of a number of aristocrats. Her aunt, after all, was a Countess. But the palace in which their King and Queen resided was something else altogether. Built by King Henry in Tudor times, but updated by successive monarchs, its reddish brick towers stood taller than Ada could see from inside the carriage.

The wings on the sides, recently added, were the best that Georgian architecture could offer and dramatically added to the scale of the palace. Unlike the lighter bricks used in modern construction, the floor to ceiling windows were fitted into brown-red stone to match the existing Tudor facade of the old palace. Ada wondered which parts were used by the royal family. Candlelight streamed from every window, even those right at the top, and yet it seemed inconceivable that the entire building could be in use.

Stepping down from the carriage, Ada walked a little behind Hetty, a shiver of nerves going through her as she took in the size and spectacle of it all. Hundreds of women more beautiful and more richly dressed than her crowded the inner courtyard and corridor, many of them awaiting their own presentation to the Queen. The older women accompanying them were no doubt many of the great ladies of the ton, here to support their daughter's entrance to society. Ada thought she recognised some of them from the illustrated fashion-plates that came in the newspapers from London.

Compared to all that, it was easy to feel small and intimidated. Ada shook off her feelings of inadequacy. It was not in her nature to be down on herself. Even Mama's constant disparaging of Ada's less than adequate looks had been insufficient to shake some core of Ada that refused to think of herself as less than anyone's equal despite her plain looks and lack of grace.

Yes, there were many young women who surpassed her in beauty and wealth, but that did not mean Ada was undeserving of affection and the comforts family could bring. Rallying herself mentally, she straightened her figure and walked confidently forward.

"Good luck Ada," whispered Hetty, pressing her hand for a moment before entering through the ballroom with Papa.

Adeline waited with her mother to be presented. It took a long time for the footman to announce them. Enough time for Ada's nerves to rear their ugly head again.

"Don't worry darling, no one is likely to pay you much heed. It's just a formality and only the prettiest girls draw any sort of attention. When Hetty came out last year, there was such a lot of fuss, but then she was one of the loveliest debutants, if I do say so myself."

Ada supposed it was some comfort to be so plain that she was below the notice of all the assembled ladies. At least no one would be likely to regard her as competition. With a bit of luck, she'd spend her season flying below the radar of the sharp-tongued gossips and meddling mamas of the ton and come out with a respectable proposal at the end. Anyway, it was really only a handful of young people who became the object of speculation each season, people like the Duke of Aberlay and last season's incomparable, Lady Selina Howard who was now Countess Stanhope. Even Hetty, for all her beauty had not been mentioned by the gossip columns. Ada had read them vociferously hoping for a mention of her sister.

"Lady Deufont, presenting her daughter, Miss Adeline Deufont."

They were finally permitted into the main chamber. The Queen, despite being a small woman, managed to instil a sense of awe and intimidation in the debutantes being presented. Somehow Ada managed to keep her head straight and her gait even and unhurried. Before the Queen at last, Ada fell into a deep curtsy. The Queen nodded and the footman called the next debutante and that was it.

Ada let out a deep breath and then a little relieved giggle. She could feel quite a few eyes fixed in her direction, but the Queen's inspection was finished, and she hadn't disgraced herself or her family in any way. Had that been what she was so worried about? Hetty had been right. There was nothing to be feared. Now she could turn her attention to her first London ball. There Ada saw little to be worried about as well. The crowd consisted of far more young women than men and it seemed unlikely that her fate as either wife or spinster would be decided this evening.

The great ballroom was split into a smaller section for the presentation of debutantes and the greater section given over to the dancing couples and orchestra. Ada managed to locate Henrietta dancing the Cotillion. Her cousin, Lavinia, who had come out the same year as Hetty, formed the other female in the four-person dance. Their male partners were unknown to Ada, although she thought she recognised one of them as Horatio Ashbourne from the gossip rags. He was reported to be one of the best-turned out dandies in England. Based on the fine cut of his waistcoat, the elaborate knot of his cravat and the shine of his boots, Ada could well believe it.

Aunt Caroline, her mother's sister, materialised before them. Even at the age of forty, Aunt Caro was beautiful, her golden hair turning silver at the temples and her eyes a clear blue. Hetty would probably look much the same at that age. Somehow standing next to her, Mama managed to look old even though she was the younger sister. Ada hoped she wouldn't look like that at the same age.

"Ada, you're officially out, isn't it wonderful," said Aunt Caro.

It didn't feel particularly wonderful. Despite her presentation being over, there were still many eyes fixed in her direction, making it hard to fully relax. Ada chalked it up to her debutante status. Hopefully it would die down soon, and she'd melt into the crowd of young, unmarried females.

"It is certainly different," Ada settled on.

"Well of course it is! Rather unusual to have the younger daughter out before the elder is married but I suppose your mother knows best."

"Having had to wait for two older sisters to wed before I came out was quite terrible enough. I have no intention of subjecting my daughters to it as well," said mother with a sniff.

Aunt Caroline coloured up. It had taken four years of rejecting proposals before the Earl of Trefasser eventually proposed to her and was gladly accepted. It had worked out well for Aunt Caro who was now a countess, but less so for Ada's mother who only came out at the age of twenty-two as a result. It was a fact that bred resentment between the sisters, particularly since mother had not been able to marry as well.

"Well, never mind," blustered Aunt Caroline, "It's a lot more common to have multiple daughters out at once nowadays. The rules are more relaxed than in the past. Why, the Earl of Morely has four daughters out together! And I know that Lady Kippering's daughters were out at the same time, before the elder got married."

"Indeed, didn't Lady William Billingsgate bring out three nieces in a single ball last season?" asked mother.

"Yes, she said she couldn't be bothered to bring them out individually," said Aunt Caroline giggling at the remembrance.

Their conversation descended into gossip concerning the ladies who were out this season and their various family connections. Ada tuned out the conversation, listening instead to the orchestra playing and watching the swirling couples on the floor. The range of instruments was far more varied with a deeper range than anything Ada had heard up to this point. She felt a thrum of delight as the low note of a harp resonated deep in her belly and the high, tinkling notes of the lyre sent a shiver of pleasure up her spine. Who knew music could be so exquisite? The musicians back at Riverstoke seemed out-of-tune and uninspired in comparison, but then the Queen would no doubt hire the best instrumentalists in the country.

It was a feast for the eyes as well as the ears. Couples swirled in time to the beats of music. Men in their dark coats contrasting against the lighter silks of the ladies they coupled.

The amount of wealth on display was staggering, women practically dripping in jewels from studded hair pins to glittering bracelets and necklaces and even the occasional jewelled slipper peeking out from beneath a silken hem. The men's adornments were more subtle but no less arresting, the glint of an ornamental watch chain visible across their hips and the occasional diamond pin fastened to their cravats that glittered dazzlingly when caught in the light. And any lack in sheer sparkle was more than made up for with the sharp cut of their clothes and unbridled use of rich fabrics.

An audible murmur rose up from the back of the ballroom and heads began to turn towards the entrance. Ada, being close to the centre of the room, was one of the last to turn her head at the spreading commotion. Standing at the top of the stairs was a Lord and Lady that Ada had no difficulty identifying. The Dowager Duchess of Aberlay and her son, the most eligible bachelor to be had in England, the Duke of Aberlay himself. The excitement that overtook a hundred mamas was tangible. So much for Hetty's pronouncement of an uneventful ball attended by only the least eligible men.

Even from a distance, Ada could see why the gossip papers wrote about him the way they did. He was handsome, no doubt, but more than that he was arresting, with piercing blue eyes and a hawk-like nose that immediately gave him a noble look. He shared with his mother, the Dowager Duchess, the darkest, midnight-black hair, although his was close-cropped in the military style. Ada remembered that he had fought on the continent before inheriting his title. A thin white scar slashed across his cheekbone served as a reminder of his military service, not that anyone was liable to forget, even though he wasn't at present wearing any of his medals.

He could at least have the decency to dress poorly, what with being handsome, a war hero and a Duke to boot. But Ada could not fault him there either. Although not quite a dandy there was a certain understated elegance in his dress. The starched, white cravat tied just so, the tight cut of his black coat highlighting the breath of his shoulders and the narrowness of his waist. He was much taller than his mother but as he descended the stairs it became clear he was taller than most of the men too.

Ada shook her head and turned from the scene. Mama and Aunt Caroline had disappeared. She looked around for them desperately. Even though she wasn't as schooled in society as Hetty, she knew she shouldn't be unchaperoned. There! She spotted them in the crowd, shoving their way through people, halfway to the Duke of Aberlay already. Ada stared after them in dismay and then realising she had little choice, picked up her skirts and followed them through the crowd as best she could.

A lot of the other mamas catching on, began to move in the direction of the Duke. But Aunt Caro and Mama were ruthless, and what's more there were two of them. They worked in tandem, elbowing and delicately shoving their way towards the Duke. Ada arrived just as her aunt and mother were coming out of a deep curtsy. She quickly dropped into a clumsy one of her own, not nearly as deep as a Duke deserved.

The Duke of Aberlay gave her a long look and Ada flushed. She'd already made a fool of herself, not that it really mattered. A Duke would have no interest in her, regardless of the depth of her curtsey. Aunt Caro who had met the Duke before, introduced them.

"My sister, Lady Duefont and her youngest daughter, Miss Adeline Duefont. His Grace, the Duke of Aberlay. Your Grace will of course remember me? You attended my ball last season," said Aunt Caro.

Ada felt her aunt was assigning the Duke far more credit than he deserved. She could visibly see the gears turning in his head as he struggled to remember who she was. "Lady Trefasser," he said after a moment too long, "How are your children?"

Aunt Caroline looked visibly pleased that the Duke remembered she had children, although Ada would wager a hundred pounds he had no idea who they were.

"My eldest, Robert, is up at Oxford and you'll recall my youngest, Lavinia, came out last year. You danced with her at the Beulle Ball. And an enchanting pair you both made. She is here tonight if you'd like to renew your acquaintance."

Her own mother was not to be outdone. "My eldest daughter was out that season as well. An exceptionally beautiful young lady if I do say so myself. I don't believe you've had the pleasure yet, Your Grace, but she is here tonight if you'd care to be introduced."

"Unfortunately, both Hetty and Lavinia are dancing the current set," said Aunt Caro, "But if Your Grace will wait a few moments, they will be done momentarily, and I am certain they will have room on their dance cards to accommodate you."

His Grace, for all his position and authority, looked overwhelmed. Ada stifled a smile. Although a war hero, clearly Aunt Caro and Mama were combatants he wasn't equipped to handle. The Duke looked around, as if for some kind of rescue, but finding the cavalry sadly lacking in the ballroom of St. James's Palace, he was forced to engineer his escape himself.

"In the meantime, Miss Adeline, will you do me the honour of the coming dance?" he asked stiffly.

Adeline had watched his struggle with a degree of amusement, wondering how he'd disengage himself. But never had she expected this. She had to admit it was genius. She had neither the breeding of Lavinia nor the beauty of Hetty to make her in any way a candidate for the Duke's hand, and so she was both a perfectly safe dance partner and a way to escape Mama and Aunt Caro.

He took her hand and led her to the edge of the dancing couples. Even though he'd only asked her to extract himself from an unwanted situation, Ada couldn't help feel a thrill to being on the arm of such a man. After all, whatever the reason, how many women could claim their first dance of the season was with the Duke of Aberlay. She flushed a bit at the barrage of stares directed their way, but the Duke strode forward confidently. His confidence gave her confidence. There was nothing to be done but meet their gazes with the same lack of concern he showed.

He stopped just outside the circle of the dance. "We'll have to wait for the set to finish. With a modicum of luck, no one will approach us," he said, his eyes scanning the surroundings as if expecting an ambush at any second.

The knowledge that the Duke was not, in any realm of possibility, a potential spouse, loosened Ada's tongue. "If Your Grace means to be in society more, you'll have to become much more adept at navigating the machinations of society matrons."

He glanced at her sideways, amusement glittering in his eyes, "Did I not just engineer a deft escape?"

"While I do not fault your quick-thinking, I won't be available every time. And any other lady you asked would attach a degree of expectation to the request. They might think you're interested in them."

"And you don't think I'm interested in you?" queried the Duke.

Ada smiled, "My elder sister, Hetty has always been the attractive one in our family. Whereas I, well, I needn't tell you that I'm no beauty. You can see it plain as day."

The Duke was silent and Ada began to regret her forthright speech. Clearly, she'd made him uncomfortable. She should have stuck to topics like the decor of the ballroom or the number of couples instead of trying to tease the man.

"Do you mean to tell me you don't think of yourself as beautiful?" he asked eventually.

"I know I am not. Not everyone can be a great beauty you know." The Duke was looking at her with a peculiar expression on his face, pity maybe. "You needn't feel sorry for me. Other than my face, which is too plain, there is nothing overtly wrong with me. I know I'm not likely to marry a title or a great fortune, but a modest gentleman will do me quite well."

"So you are angling after neither my fortune nor title?"

"I am no fool, Your Grace. There is no way on earth you would be prevailed upon to marry the daughter of a baronet. You are a Duke. The difference in our stations is too great."

"You are good ton, aren't you? Your aunt is a Countess."

"Oh yes, mother's relations are all very well connected. Her father is a Baron. But that can mean little to you when you have your pick of any one of the most eligible ladies of the ton. Isn't the Duke of Norfolk's daughter out?"

The Duke visibly shuddered, "Lady Charlotte. Don't remind me."

"What's the matter with her?"

"A terrible snob," said the Duke, leaning closer, "Thinks being a Duke's relation gives her more consequence and thus treats everyone accordingly."

"Do you really mean to tell me a Duke's relations aren't better than everyone else?" she asked teasingly.

He laughed, a delightful, rich sound that vibrated through Ada. "What am I saying? I rescind my criticism of Lady Charlotte and furthermore, as she's the only marriageable woman equal to my lofty station I shall begin my official courtship of her tomorrow."

Ada laughed, she couldn't help herself. The Duke looked at her suddenly, turning his attention away from the room. With difficulty Ada stopped, bringing a gloved hand up to her mouth to muffle the sound. Her laugh had always been a source of embarrassment to her. Deep and throaty and not at all light and airy like a young woman's should be. Like Hetty's was.

"You needn't silence yourself on my account," he said.

"You don't mind my laugh? Mama always said it was unladylike and that men would dislike me for it."

"How little your mother knows of men. Your laugh is delicious. Most women just simper in the most annoying fashion."

"Like this?" said Ada, raising the pitch of her voice and tittering between her teeth.

"No, it's more like this," said the Duke. To Ada's delight he drew a deep breath and let out a girlish giggle that sounded identical to that of most young ladies. He continued in a high falsetto voice, "Oh, Your Grace, how handsome you are, and how intelligent, and how heroic. If I keep flattering you and giggling like this," he let out another convincingly girlish laugh, "why, then you'll surely make me a Duchess," he finished.

Beside him, Ada was almost in tears from laughing so hard, her sides hurting with the effort. The Duke smiled at her wickedly. A smile that sent Ada's heart quickening despite herself.

"Oh dear, you must stop or I shall be out of breath before we get to actually dancing," she said.

"Well then, Miss Adeline, we'd better begin," said the Duke, taking her hand and leading her forward just as the last set ended and the signal was given for the next. Ada caught a glimpse of a wide-eyed Hetty staring at her as she left the floor. Not only was her sister completely wrong about no one of importance showing up, neither of them in a million years could have imagined Adeline would step out with the Duke of Aberlay himself. The easiness she'd felt just moments ago dissipated as Ada sharply remembered who she was dancing with.

It was not only Hetty's eyes on her either. It seemed the entire ballroom was paying attention to the Duke's chosen dance partner. A quick glance around proved this to be true, as more than a few eyes slid away upon making contact with hers.

"Do they always stare at you like this?" she asked.

"I think in this instance they are staring more at you than me," he said.

"That is of little comfort."

"Don't mind them. Keep your eyes on me," he said, slipping his arm around her. The Duke's hold was nothing like the boys she'd danced with in Riverstoke, it was confident and commanding and instantly made her feel safe, even as a thrill shot through her spine. Until this moment, she had never understood how intimate dancing could be. Ada heated up, acutely aware of all the points of contact between them. She placed her free hand, the one not held by his, on his shoulder and raised her eyes to meet his.

Their gazes locked and the rest of the world blurred into insignificance.

He led her smoothly and effortlessly through a vigorous set, showing little signs of exertion even as Ada felt her heart begin to pick up pace and her leg muscles work to keep up the quick half-steps and high skips of the traditional English country dance. It was a pleasure to be led by such a skilled partner. The Duke never faltered either in the steps or their pacing, keeping himself and Ada effortlessly in time with the rhythms of the orchestra.

The harp began to thrum faster and faster. Pure exhilaration coursed through Ada as the Duke tightened his grip ever so imperceptibly and spun her around, guiding her through the final, faster paced section of the dance. Even he was showing signs of exertion now, both of them breathing deeper as they moved about the floor. His muscled thighs brushed against her leg repeatedly, sending little shivers of pleasure through her at the illicit touch. And he held her so close, Ada could feel the heat from his large body. His eyes remained fixed on hers the entire time, and Ada couldn't look away, her heart pounding in her chest and not just from the vigour of the dance.

He spun her around into the final position, and they froze with the other dancers, arms raised above their heads as they panted against each other, gazes locked. The string instruments sounded out their final long note in a moment that seemed to go on for eternity as their arms slowly dropped and around them couples began to separate. Ada was gripped with a sudden urge to never let go, a desire to dance the next set and the next set with the Duke until they were both too tired to dance again. But awareness of their surroundings slowly creeped in and with it the unwelcome realisation that this odd feeling was entirely one sided. She would likely never dance with the Duke again.

The orchestra fell to silence and Ada tugged her hand out of the Duke's still firm grip. She curtsied, forcing him to return a bow and managed to plaster a smile onto her face, "I won't keep you any longer, Your Grace," she said, walking away before he could reply with some polite platitude he wouldn't mean.

Chapter 4
An Obligation to Dance

Kit watched Adeline Duefont walk away with a small rustle of her dress and a slight sway of her hips. A gleam of white shoulders, glossy hair and sparkling sapphires, she passed easily through the men who moved aside for her, unconscious of their admiring gazes upon her figure and face. A stunningly beautiful woman, even if the lady didn't think so herself. She seemed to bring all the glamour and grace of the world with her as she moved across the room and Kit stared helplessly after her, enraptured.

He couldn't believe himself in love after a single dance, he would like to think he possessed more good sense and intelligence than that. But it would be useless to deny to himself that he was interested in Miss Adeline Duefont. Certainly, some long hidden part of himself had responded to her. He might even go so far as to claim himself captivated. It was already far more than he'd ever felt for any other woman.

The Duke laughed to himself. What would his mother say? Him the Duke of Aberlay, the most admired man amongst them, admiring a girl more unsophisticated and of lower breeding than the hundreds of debutants she'd introduced him to over the years. How antagonising for her that the only woman to invoke sentimental feelings in him was one his dear mother hadn't seen fit to include in her many matchmaking soirées and dinner parties. Speak of the devil. His mother materialised beside him, finished with her introduction to the Queen.

"Who was that lady you were dancing the quartet with?" his mother enquired, apropos of any kind of greeting.

The woman had eyes in the back of her head. "Some girl I had to stand up with as she was unpartnered when we were introduced," he said mildly.

The Dowager Duchess gave a grunt of dissatisfaction. "These pushy mamas forcing introductions with their daughters. I hope it wasn't too tedious for you."

It hadn't been tedious at all. In fact, he might even go as far as to say his dance partner was amongst the loveliest example of her sex, a diamond amongst a sea of semi-precious rocks. But he knew better than to actually say any of that. It was sickeningly flowery, a prize-winning poet he was not. Moreover, the last thing he needed was to draw his mother's attention towards a fleeting attraction when he was trying to stifle her matchmaking impulses.

"Have you met Lady Edith and Lady Esther, the daughters of the Earl of Watterford?" his mother continued, "I see their mother waving at me now. Come." She grabbed his arm and tugged him none too gently towards where the insipid ladies and their mama waited. "Their mother is a daughter of the Marquess of Harringate so the ladies are of remarkably good breeding. They are both of similar age which is why their mother has seen fit to have them out at the same time. An increasingly popular trend, and one I'm not sure I entirely approve of."

The ladies had already begun to giggle at his approach. With difficulty Kit resisted rolling his eyes and instead kept his face carefully blank. Forget medals of valour for war service, instead they should hand out awards for stoically bearing the simpering of silly young women at parties like this. He would much rather face the bayonets of Napoleon's forces than the fluttering eyelashes and sickly-sweet flattery of debutants wishing to marry his title and fortune. But unfortunately, his mother was as formidable as any general and moreover was shamelessly willing to use his affection for her to get him to go along with her schemes.

"Lady Watterford, I don't believe you've met my son," said Mama, gesturing towards him.

"Your Grace, I of course know who you are," the lady in question flushed, "that is -"

"Charmed." said Kit quickly, cutting her off. He bowed in her direction, perhaps a little lower than required considering his status as a Duke and hers as a Countess, but he'd leave it to his mother and sister to measure the degrees of a bow and who was deserving of a few inches more or less.

The lady, despite being over forty at least, blushed as readily as any maid. Either that or the whole family was plagued with rosacea. Which was a distinct possibility considering that both her offspring sported similarly reddened cheeks. Her daughters tittered beside her in a way Kit supposed was meant to be endearing but instead was highly irritating. Neither girl was particularly pretty, though they'd tried to make up for it with expensive jewels and an excessive use of lace ruffles.

"May I present my daughters, Edith and Esther. Edith is a fantastic pianist and Esther a charming lute player. Her instructor says she plays as beautifully as one of the Greek muses."

"And which muse would that be? Thalia perhaps?" he said, naming the muse of comedy.

His mother's eyes narrowed in his direction, but none of the other women picked up on the insult. Kit sighed internally, clearly reading was not one of the ladies' accomplishments.

"Oh, Your Grace, you are so terribly clever! Why other than being compared to one once, I cannot say I have ever heard anything about the muses. Perhaps you would be kind enough to educate me? My next dance slot is free." This statement was accompanied by a determined flutter of the lashes.

This one must be Esther then, the lute player. What she lacked in intelligence, she clearly made up for in boldness and cunning. It would be very difficult for him to refuse politely and judging by her smug expression and the put-out pouting of her sister, he was not the only one to have realised it.

He put on his most charming smile. Might as well get the inevitable over with, he wasn't getting out of this without offering at least one set. "Perhaps then Lady Esther, we might discuss Greek Literature over the next dance."

Her sister's pout developed into a full-blown frown. Esther smiled so widely that he could see her molars. "Why Your Grace, I'd be delighted to accept!" She thrust her fan at her sister to hold and was clutching at his arm in seconds.

For such a little lady she certainly had a firm grip.

"Are you familiar with Sophocles or Euripedes who wrote Media?" he asked in an attempt to keep his word. They were popular Greek plays and perhaps the lady might at least be familiar with them through the theatre if not a book.

She glanced up at him with a sugary expression, "I'm afraid not, Your Grace. How many great and important things you must know due to your position. I cannot claim to be anywhere near as knowledgeable as you. Indeed, I doubt any man of the ton can," she said, ending this extraordinary statement with a titter.

"I assure you Lady Esther, any gentleman of the ton has access to the same reading material as I, and many of them are vastly more knowledgeable on the subject of the Greek plays." As are many of the women, although you are clearly not one of them, he added in his head.

That annoying titter again. "If you say so, Your Grace."

He bowed to her to begin the set. The dance was less vigorous than the one he'd danced with Miss Adeline, so unfortunately talking was a distinct possibility. He wished the sets had been reversed, he would much prefer conversing with his previous partner than his current one. Thankfully, the movements of the reel, weaving in and out of other couples in the dance, at least meant that contact between them was minimal. That didn't stop Lady Esther from prattling on though, flattering him and making herself look daft in equal turn. Were there really gentlemen who found this sort of attention agreeable? Perhaps men who had little self-confidence in themselves or their positions might find the constant stream of syrupy compliments gratifying. But Kit was in no need of having his ego stoked, and he found it highly irritating instead.

After an age, the dance came to an end and Kit escorted the young lady back to where her mother and sister waited. He saw that his own mother had fled the scene. Clearly the Dowager Duchess was quite willing to subject him to company she herself wouldn't put up with.

At his approach, the other daughter, Lady Emillia or something, began to open her mouth to speak, but he wasn't about to be caught a second time.

"I think I see an old university friend. Excuse me ladies," he said quickly. Bowing, he turned and walked in the opposite direction as abruptly as possible without actually running.

It wasn't a lie exactly, but certainly a convenient excuse. He'd spotted his old friend, Manderville, lounging around the edges of the ballroom, studiously avoiding eye-contact with any of the enterprising mamas or eager debutants trying to get his attention. As a young and unattached Viscount, he was just as liable to be swarmed by marriage-minded ladies as Kit himself, despite his reputation as a rake.

"Manderville!"

"Well look what the devil dragged in," said Manderville in that slow, sardonic way of his, "I'd say you're eager to see me, but based on that last dance partner, I'd guess you're more happy to have an excuse to escape."

"Lord Watterford's daughters. You've had the pleasure?"

"The delightful Edith and Esther. One plays the piano, the other the lute, and neither has a brain between them."

Kit couldn't help but smile at the apt description. "I see you're well acquainted. One of them coerced me into a dance. They had brains enough for that at least."

"Oh, I don't deny that they're in possession of some base cunning, the way you might observe in more intelligent animals, but little more than that. The snub-nosed one, Edith, actually thought Beethovan was a painter when I mentioned he was the greatest artist of our time."

"Beethovan? Really? How on earth did you react?"

Manderville gave him a devilish grin, "I told her I thought his use of colour surpassed the Baroque period and that his brushwork was the equal of Botticelli. And of course, she completely agreed with me."

Kit shook his head even as he laughed at the image of a studiously solemn Manderville waxing poetic about the great Beethovan's painting style, the Lady Edith nodding along vacantly to his pack of lies.

"It begs the question, what on earth does she play on that piano of hers?"

Manderville winced, "Pray that we never find out Kit. Demonstrations of debutant talents are best avoided, like the plague or venereal disease."

"Well, you would know all about that. What are you doing here in the most staid event of the season, rather than in the bed of one of your paramours?"

"Same thing you are in all likelihood. We've been brow beaten into it by our mothers. Mine is sponsoring the coming out of some second cousin twice removed. Poor girl is about as attractive as the rear end of a horse. Mother was scared no one would dance with her, which is why I was dragged along, to do the honours." Manderville's expression indicated that he didn't consider it much of an honour at all.

"Shouldn't you be standing up with her now then? You've missed a set already while we've been talking."

"You probably didn't notice, since your partner for the first dance was actually quite lovely. But I was not so lucky. While you were twirling that elegant creature around, I was escorting the not-so-lovely Horatia across the dance floor. My duty done, I deposited her with the other wallflowers where she belongs and I dare say that's where she'll remain for the rest of the night."

Kit followed Manderville's gaze to the edge of the dance-floor. The woman in question was indeed unfortunate in appearance. Her eyes were unsymmetrical, one sitting slightly higher on her face than the other and her mouth hung perpetually open as if the weight of her fleshy jaw weighed the lower half of her face down. She stood shyly beside Manderville's mother, the Dowager Viscountess, as if aware of her own unattractive appearance. Kit felt rather sorry for her. Manderville's assessment was right. She wasn't likely to be asked to dance by anyone else tonight.

"Who was that delightful creature you accompanied in the first set anyway?" asked Manderville.

Kit's eyes unwittingly slid to Miss Adeline where she was being led in the quadrille by yet another gentleman. Without realising it, he'd maintained an awareness of her movements the whole night and as soon as Manderville asked after her, he'd known exactly where to look. It was her third dance partner of the night. Not that he was keeping count. Unlike the unfortunate Horatia, Adeline had danced every set. He found himself, yet again, admiring the classic beauty of her figure. She wore a short-waisted, dainty dress made of silk thin enough to glimpse an outline of the shapely form of her legs as she skipped in time to the reel. A particularly vigorous hop had her skirt hem flick up just enough for him to glimpse a well-turned ankle clad in sheer stockings. To his surprise, Kit felt himself begin to harden in his breeches.

Manderville snapped his fingers in front of Kit's face, startling him out of his reverie. His friend had a far too knowing smirk upon his face.

"Never thought I'd see the day," said Manderville in that slow drawl of his.

"It's nothing," said Kit too quickly.

Impossibly Manderville's smirk grew wider. Kit had all but confirmed what Manderville suspected. But thankfully his friend didn't push it, and Kit knew unlike some people he wouldn't spread it around. Manderville was nothing if not discrete.

"I think we've both endured enough of this to satisfy our mothers. I'm off to White's. Care to join me for a drink?" asked Manderville.

"I'll meet you there shortly, save me a seat. First, I'm going to ask poor Horatia to dance," replied Kit.

Manderville shook his head, "You're a bleeding-heart, Kit. Luckily, my conscience is far less well-developed than yours. I'll see you at White's." And with a firm thump on Kit's shoulder, Manderville was out the door as swiftly as a hound out the kennel.

The Dowager Viscountess eagerly introduced Kit to Miss Horatia Neville. The poor girl was so grateful she thanked him three times, and while she had an unfortunate stammer, her conversation was quite polite and sensible, a trait which made her vastly preferable to Lady Esther. After depositing her back with the Dowager Viscountess, he noticed another gentleman approaching to ask Horatia for the next set, the attention of a Duke elevating her from wallflower to a person of interest.

While his sense of compassion might be better honed than Manderville's, it was not endless. His good deed done, he made a beeline for the door, assiduously avoiding the gazes of the many mamas and debutants trying to catch his eye. He looked back one last time before the door shut, and caught a last glimpse of Adeline, her head thrown back in laughter and her dark hair loose around her face from hours of dancing. It was her fifth set. Not that he was counting.

Chapter 5
A Morning in London

"His Grace, The Duke of Aber-"

"For God's sake, Burnley, you needn't announce me every time I visit my own mother," said Kit, brushing past the butler and into The Dowager Duchess's morning room where breakfast had just been laid out.

"Very good, Your Grace," said the butler with a sniff, bowing as he left the room.

"You mustn't be too harsh on him dear, your father was something of a stickler for protocol and his influence still lingers in the older servants," said his mother, presenting her cheek for a kiss.

Kit obliged before grabbing a fluffy scone from the pastry dish and smearing it liberally with butter. He took a moment to study his mother. She looked better rested than anyone should be after the first ball of the season. Scattered before her was what looked like every single gossip rag in London.

"What on earth are you reading that swill for?" he asked.

"Just seeing if anything noteworthy happened last night that I missed. All the women you danced with are mentioned by name."

"How gratifying," said Kit dryly.

"Of the three women singled out by the Duke of Aberlay," began the Dowager Duchess, reading from the paper, "any one of those ladies would make fine Duchesses, all of impeccable breeding and remarkable social grace. This writer, and for that matter, the whole of England, waits with bated breath to see who the Duke will choose to be his Duchess."

"How quickly these gossip columns jump from a single dance to matrimony," said Kit, brushing breadcrumbs off his coat, "I particularly liked the part about 'remarkable social grace', I didn't realise this was a comedy rag."

His mother's mouth twitched, "Yes Lady Esther is a bit of a bore, isn't she? Won't you stay and have a proper breakfast, I'll ring for Burnley to send a plate up for you."

"Can't," said Kit, swallowing his pastry, "They're approving funding in the House of Lords for the war today. I need to read through the papers. It's the least I can do to help those men fighting in France." There was an undertone of guilt colouring Kit's words that his mother picked up immediately.

"Oh darling, you've already done so much. Far more than most men in your position. How many peers of the realm have been to the battle fields, fought alongside the soldiers, put their lives at risk?"

"Viscount Wellington, for one."

"Pfft, he was ennobled for his military service, he was a title-less gentleman before the war and had to make his fortune somehow. You already stood to inherit a Dukedom and a vast fortune and you risked it all to defend your country."

"Well, I am risking nothing now, safely at home in England attending silly parties and dinner functions. The least I can do is make sure the men fighting to defend us are well-supplied and properly equipped."

"My darling boy, always taking on the responsibilities of the world. You came into the Dukedom at such a young age, and now you're arguing in parliament for the defence of England. There are men twice your age who do less."

Kit grabbed another scone for the carriage ride brushing off the compliments. He did his duty, nothing more, "I really must go. Give my regards to Marianne if you see her. She's arriving today, isn't she?"

"Yes, little Peter made a full recovery, so there's nothing stopping your sister from partaking in the full London season, minus last night's ball of course. Lord Reeth is already here. I believe you'll see him in parliament today."

"I'm afraid so. Marianne's husband makes a point of opposing most of my policies," said Kit with a wince.

"I have every faith in your ability to win him, and all the rest of them, over to your side."

Kit was less sure. No matter how prettily or passionately he spoke, the majority of the chamber came in already firmly decided on which way they would vote. He needed to convince that exceedingly rare demographic, the undecided voter.

The chamber's benches were already half-full and filling up fast when Kit walked in. Understandable given the importance of the issue. None of the Lords wanted to give the impression they didn't care about soldiers at the front. Kit shuffled his papers, taking a last quick look through his notes before getting up to speak. He was no great orator, so he strived for simplicity and hoped his testimony and the truth of his words would do the convincing that his rhetoric could not. He told the gathered Lords of his own experience during the war, the lack of warm clothes for the common soldier and the meanness of the rations that left men marching on unsatisfied stomachs.

"These men, much abused and much beleaguered, sent to foreign lands to fight for us, deserve every ounce of support we can give. Whilst English blood is spilt on French soil, will this house do less than give our soldiers its unwavering and unequivocal support? Because make no mistake, my fellow lords, a rejection of this bill is a slap to the face to every man who has served and bled on the continent in defence of our freedom. I implore you, lend your support to this legislation and show your determination to defeat once and for all the scourge that is Napoleon."

He sat down to rousing cheers. Hopefully framing the issue as one of either opposing or supporting Napoleon would make it difficult for his fellow members to vote against. It seemed inconceivable to him that there were those who would baulk at sending funding to English soldiers fighting to defend their country. But here was one of them, standing up to speak now. Kit narrowed his eyes at his brother-in-law. The Marquess of Reeth walked unhurriedly to the dispatch box with the conviction of a man who knew he had the undivided attention of the entire house.

Kit hadn't been lying earlier when he'd said the man seemed to make a point of arguing against almost everything Kit supported. He knew his sister, Marianne, and Lord Reeth didn't have a particularly happy marriage, but sometimes, in parliament, it felt like his brother-in-law took it out on him. It didn't help either that he was over a decade older than Kit and had spent most of that time honing his oratory abilities. Lord Reeth was a talented and experienced politician and Kit wished he wasn't so consistently on the side of the opposition.

"The supporters of this expensive bill will try and frame this debate as one of patriotism," began Lord Reeth, his confident tones echoing through the chamber, "They tell you that unless you pass this legislation through parliament, you are registering your support for that vile dictator across the sea. I tell you today, that I am as keen as any of you here, to see the reign of Napoleon ended. But I do not believe that his defeat will be achieved by vast sums of gold flowing out of the Royal Treasury and into France, sums of money so vast they threaten to bankrupt our nation."

Kit could almost feel the political mood turning as Lord Reeth spun a tale of profligate spending and bloated army budgets. It was true there was a degree of wasteful spending in the army, that was true of any large organisation, but more funding did actually ensure that more went towards better equipment and supplies. To hear Lord Reeth tell it though, whatever money parliament gave to the army would simply be squandered and have no impact on the outcome of the war. The lie made Kit's blood boil, his fists clenched, wanting to punch something, preferably Lord Reeth's mouth. He was a man used to actual battlefields, not the verbal sparring of political theatre.

"Easy there, old friend, don't want to get us both thrown out," said Manderville, eyeing Kit's clenched fists. Manderville normally had more important things to do than attend parliamentary sessions, at least things he deemed more important, but he'd made an exception to listen to Kit's speech and vote on this issue.

With difficulty Kit relaxed his muscles, "Why would you get thrown out if I punched Lord Reeth?"

"Well, you'd almost certainly be dragged off him, which would put me in the terribly inconvenient position of having to jump in to defend you," said Manderville with his characteristic nonchalance, "So be a chum and save me the trouble, would you. Besides, I doubt your sister would be pleased if you punched her husband in public."

"Actually, I think Marianne would like to punch him herself a few times," said Kit.

"Oh, I don't doubt it, and I'm sure Marianne could land a punch just as well as you, but I think she'd more object to the fighting in parliament bit. By all means go at it all you want with Lord Reeth in private, I won't lift a finger to stop you, but your mother and sister will have something to say about a public punch up between their two closest male relatives. Just imagine what tomorrow's papers would make of it."

Kit shuddered at the thought of their combined verbal haranguing. Unfortunately for him, his status as Duke was no deterrent against the two women who'd known him as a snot-nosed baby. His mother was bad enough without having to contend with his older sister too, "You make an excellent point. Marianne's just arrived in London so I would be directly in both their firing ranges, so to speak."

"Marianne's in London, how wonderful! I shall have to call on her and the children. Did she bring them up with her from Dorset?"

"Almost certainly. Peter was unwell, one of those illnesses children are always coming down with. He's better now, but I still doubt Marianne would wish to be parted from him. And of course, if Peter is coming up, she could hardly leave little Isabella behind."

"Marianne has such a wonderful maternal instinct about her, quite unlike most women of the ton," said Manderville admiringly.

Kit chose not to reply to that. He hoped Manderville's appreciation was entirely platonic. He'd often wondered about the relationship between his sister and his friend. The Viscount had a reputation for bedding unhappily married women and Marianne definitely fell into that category. Whatever was going on between them, friendship or something more, Kit was happier not knowing. It wasn't his business anyway. His sister was married. It was her husband's job now to defend her honour, so at the very least, Kit would never find himself in the uncomfortable situation of having to duel his closest friend.

"Best of luck, Kittrington," whispered Manderville, standing up.

Kit realised with a start that Lord Reeth had returned to his bench and voting on the bill had begun. There was nothing more to be done except hope the result went in his favour.

In the bright sunshine outside, the stifling tension prevailing in the dark halls of parliament lost their grip on Kit and he felt his shoulders relax. Sailing vessels travelled down the Thames and children played in the riverbank, chasing each other around and making mud pies by slapping the sodden earth together under their small palms. The sounds of their mirth travelled up parliament hill, and suddenly the day seemed full of promise.

"Think you'll get a win?" asked Manderville next to him.

"I think we might just eke one out," replied Kit, with a smile.

"I hope so. I got out of bed early for this. And now I'm going right back into it," said Manderville, raising his arm for his carriage to be pulled up.

"I appreciate your sacrifice," said Kit, mock solemnly.

"Yes, yes, we can't all be military men trained to get up at the crack of dawn or whatever ungodly hour they had you rising at," said Manderville, ducking into his carriage and tugging down the curtain. Clearly his friend held far less appreciation for the sun than Kit did.

"Shall I get your carriage pulled up, Your Grace?" asked one of the parliamentary runners.

"No, thank you, I prefer to walk. Though I'd appreciate it if you would let them know," he said, tossing a half-crown the boy's way and turning in the opposite direction to the coaches.

With his long strides, Kit ate up the length of the narrow road running north from Westminster. The imposing structures on either side of the street, a mixture of the old medieval palace and the newer Georgian buildings were enough to make even a Duke feel inconsequential. Each of their long glass windows stretched beyond the height of any man, effigies of angels and historic figures competed with each other for attention, and all around him the weight of history settled.

He turned into the open space of St. James' Park, intending to continue right towards Mayfair, but instead his feet travelled straight through into Green Park and past the narrow strip of residential houses that separated the two smaller gardens from the great green expanse of Hyde Park. Sweet chestnuts and English oaks stood as tall in central London as they'd ever grown outside it, their knotty branches beginning to bud with the leaves of spring.

It was late enough in the morning for the fashionable set to begin emerging from their townhouses and ladies in wide-brimmed hats and parasols were already promenading around the park, some of them accompanied by well-heeled suitors, while anxious mamas hovered a few feet away. He told himself he'd come to see if Marianne was about. After all, fresh air would likely do his recuperating nephew some good. But the other reason, the one that sent his pulse racing, was the hope of seeing Adeline Duefont again.

Every dark-haired lady gave him pause, made him look twice, but none of them under their hats had her eyes or her upturned nose or that delicate rosebud of a mouth that always seemed on the verge of a smile. And then he caught sight of her, standing awkwardly in a party of three. She was simply dressed, in white muslin and a straw bonnet that belonged more on a countryside hike than the fashionable promenading of Hyde Park, and yet that did nothing to detract from her striking looks. He had vaguely hoped he'd misremembered his reaction to her. That what he'd felt last night had been due to the darkness of the ballroom or some spell wrought by the music and lights. But in the harsh glare of daylight, she was unbelievably, even more beautiful, and Kit was filled with a visceral want.

He was staring at her when she noticed him, and Kit had to mentally kick himself into some kind of coherent response when she nodded in his direction.

"Miss Adeline," he managed to get out.

Her two companions turned to look at him. He recognised Mr. Ashbourne, the younger brother of Viscount Beulle, and the other woman could only be Adeline's sister from the similarities between them. She was undoubtedly pretty, but her paler colouring did her no favours, and there was something lacking in the composition of her features, an extra slant of the eyes, a lack of definition in the jaw, a thinness in the lips that was all perfected in Adeline. How Adeline could consider herself anything less than shockingly beautiful was beyond his ability to grasp, he was finding it difficult to pay attention to her companions with her in front of him.

"My sister, Miss Henrietta Deufont and Mr Ashbourne. His Grace, the Duke of Aberlay," said Adeline introducing them.

He managed to turn his gaze away from her long enough to nod in their direction and bow slightly to her sister.

"Your arrival is fortuitous, Your Grace," said Henrietta, "We've just bumped into Mr Ashbourne and thought to take a walk around the park, but three is an awkward number to walk abreast. If you accompany Ada, then we could walk more easily in pairs. That is if you don't have any prior engagements?"

He took an immediate liking to Henrietta Duefont, who seemed to have no interest in fawning over him, and moreover had given him the opportunity to spend time with her sister.

"I have no prior engagements," he said, offering his arm to the dark-haired lady beside him. Her small hand gripped him and he felt an undeniable thrill at the contact. He was no schoolboy to be jumping at the briefest contact with a woman and yet here he was, excited by her mere presence.

He allowed Mr Ashbourne and Henrietta to walk on a bit before following, the gravel path crunching beneath them with each step. It was a cloudless day and the sun shone brightly in a noble attempt to keep the inhabitants of London warm.

"Your sister calls you Ada?' he remarked, searching for something to say.

"My whole family does. It is less cumbersome than 'Adeline'. What does your family call you? I can't imagine your mother says, *His Grace, the Duke of Aberlay* every time she wishes to get your attention?"

He laughed, "No, indeed she does not, nor do most people who know me well. To them I simply go by Kit."

"Kit?" She furrowed her nose in confusion, and he found it so adorable he had to laugh again.

"What's wrong with Kit? It's certainly not cumbersome," he said teasingly.

She blushed slightly, and he found that endearing too. "Only, shouldn't everyone call you Aberlay? Or Duke? That is your title after all and that's how most men with titles tend to be called by friends."

He liked that she challenged him. If she'd been one of those simpering women who agreed with everything he said it might have been easier to forget her.

"Before I became the Duke of Aberlay, I was known by its subsidiary title, the Marquess of Kittrington. I was Kittrington at birth and through my school days and my military career, brief as it was. So, most people who knew me then, before I became a Duke, call me Kit."

"The Marquess of Kittrington, His Grace, the Duke of Aberlay, so many different names for a single man!"

"It gets worse, I am also the Earl of Edgeforth, Viscount Ames, Baron Wolsley and Baron Decraw. And all that is on top of my given name, James Bartholemew Ruthmoore."

Adeline shook her head, sending the curls bouncing under her bonnet. "It makes me sad that I only have one. 'Adeline Duefont' seems positively boring in comparison. How unfair that great men get a paragraph of names to choose from and women are stuck with no selection at all."

"Women can have just as many names. For example, if we were to marry, you would be styled Her Grace, the Duchess of Aberlay, and you could lay claim to Marchioness Kittrington, Countess Edgeforth, Viscountess Ames, etcetera." Too late, he realised what he'd said. Was he really thinking of marriage so quickly? His heart, already unsteady in her presence, sped up. Luckily, she seemed not to notice.

"I suppose great ladies like your mother do indeed have grand titles. It seems everyone in your family does. Your sister is a Marchioness as well if I recall correctly. How tiresome it must be for someone to greet all of you together by all your many names."

He couldn't keep the grin off his face. "Well, you needn't not address me for fear it will be tiresome. I would be very happy to be called Kit by you."

"Oh. Well then. I suppose you must call me Adeline or Ada. That is only fair. But only in private. The gossip rags are awful already without anyone hearing us on such familiar terms. Much more of it and the ton's eligible bachelors will be scared away."

The thought was disturbingly pleasing. "Are the young men of the ton so easily frightened?"

"To hear my mother tell it, the slightest faux pas from a young lady is enough to send them running. So, either young men are not very brave, or women are terrifying creatures. I have not decided which yet."

"I think I know which one it is," he said with a smile.

They'd walked away from the gravel path, across the grass and towards the trees that lined the perimeter of London's premier park. Waiting on the road, ready to take them away was a shiny barouche with the hood down, pulled by a pair of elegant Cleveland Bays.

Kit recognised the crest on the door as Viscount Beulle's. It made sense for Mr. Ashbourne to borrow his brother's coach. Keeping a carriage and team of horses in London was an unnecessary expense for a single man of limited means. He approved. It was frustrating to see young men going into debt to finance flashy thoroughbreds and high-perch phaetons. Then he smiled at himself. He was not so 'old' himself to go about clucking after the habits of 'young' men. Mr. Ashbourne and he were likely of an age.

"Can we offer you a ride, Your Grace?" asked Mr. Ashbourne.

"No, thank you. I'm in a mood to walk."

He had much to think on. And anyway, talking to Adeline wouldn't be the same with her sister and Mr. Ashbourne listening to every word.

Most of the time, Kit was a serious person, cold even, some might say. The untimely death of his father had thrust him into a Dukedom at an age when most men were still finishing university, and the sudden responsibility had meant he'd had to mature faster than his peers. But with Ada, even in such a brief interaction, he felt a different version of himself emerge. If he had to examine it, he'd say he was filled with a newly found excitement for life, a sudden jolt of happiness that he'd not expected but was nonetheless not unwelcome. It was odd, unbalancing, something he would feel embarrassed to admit to. An infatuation with a debutante. But God, what a debutante.

Chapter 6
What Happens at Night

Clank. Clank. Ada awoke to strange noises. A pebble being thrown at glass and then after a while, the rapid rustling of skirts. She blearily opened her eyes and saw a masked Hetty with one leg out the window.

"Hetty! What on earth are you doing?"

Hetty glanced at Ada, then back out the window, then back to Ada again. As her eyes adjusted to the darkness, she noticed her sister was wearing a white mask that covered most of her face with a matching domino, a long cloak-like garment draped over a dress. The whole ensemble was incredibly risqué.

"I don't suppose you'll go back to sleep and forget you ever saw me?" tried Hetty.

"Not a chance," said Ada, jumping out of bed, "What are you thinking sneaking off in the middle of the night with God-knows-who? If someone recognises you, your reputation will be ruined! And don't try and tell me you're going to a respectable event. You would be leaving through the door not the window if that were the case!"

Out of the two of them, Ada had always been the more responsible. Mama was more tolerant of Hetty's foibles and made allowances for behaviour she would never permit with Ada. But this was a step above not wearing a hat outdoors or forgetting one's gloves. Her sister could get in serious trouble.

Hetty crossed the room to Ada and took her hands in hers. "I'm not sneaking off with someone disreputable. Well, I am sneaking, but he's not disreputable. It's Mr. Ashbourne. You've met him. You know he's an honourable man."

"Mr. Ashbourne?"

"The truth is Ada, I love him. I have since my first season in London."

Ada pulled back in shock. But Hetty continued undettered.

"We wish to marry, but Mama won't allow it and Papa listens to everything she says. She even disapproves of me seeing him, like today at Hyde Park.

You heard what she said about him at dinner."

Ada winced at the remembrance. Mama hadn't minced her words, she'd as good as called Mr. Ashbourne a fortune hunter and made it clear he had no business 'sniffing around her daughters.' Luckily, the Duke of Aberlay's surprise appearance mollified Mama somewhat and she was more convinced than ever that Hetty had a chance with the Duke.

"You see why I have to sneak about and use subterfuge?" said Hetty, "Oh, it makes me miserable that we can't be together properly. Please don't stop me, Ada. Horatio won't let any harm come to me."

"He was one of the suitors who proposed marriage last season?" asked Ada.

Hetty nodded miserably. Well, that was something. At least Mr. Ashbourne seriously intended to wed Hetty and he wasn't just playing with her sister's feelings. From what Ada had seen of the man, he seemed of good character, but he lacked both the fortune and title their mother craved and was unlikely to inherit either.

"Alright, but I am coming with you," said Ada. She could believe her sister infatuated, but to imagine flighty, easy-going Hetty in love was harder to swallow. Her sister might trust this man, but Ada didn't know him well enough to. Hopefully her being there as chaperone would stop Hetty from doing anything too stupid and stave off some of the scandal if they did get caught.

Hetty began to protest, but Ada was unmoved. Clank. Another pebble clattered across their windowpane. Hetty glanced anxiously outside. "Oh, very well," said Hetty, faced with an unwavering Ada and an impatient Mr. Ashbourne below, "but you can't very well go dressed like that."

Going to her chest, Hetty rummaged briefly before pulling out a black dress with matching domino and mask. "I wore this for a masquerade ball last season. Oh, don't look at me like that Ada, it was a respectable ball held by Lady Tweedsgate. Mama and Papa were even there. No, don't bother with a corset. There isn't time. The dress has inbuilt support anyway and the domino will hide your chest."

Ada blushed as she slipped the dress over nothing but her chemise. The garment's support didn't extend to cover her breasts but instead ended just below them, serving to push up her cleavage but doing nothing to conceal the shape of each breast and nipple. She hastily tugged the cape-like domino over her shoulders and found with relief it covered her entire chest from view. She tied the mask around her head and had time for a quick glance in the mirror to make sure everything was in place, before Hetty was dragging her out the window.

"Come on, we can fix everything in the carriage," said Hetty, climbing down the tall sycamore that branched to their window.

She wouldn't be fixing anything in front of Mr. Ashbourne other than her mask, thought Ada privately as she followed Hetty in scampering down the tree.

"Adeline's coming with us," said Hetty to a masked man who must be Mr. Ashbourne.

He took this information with remarkably little protest and soon their carriage was racing down the moonlit streets of London. Purple-grey shadows sped past the window, interspersed by the occasional yellow glow of a streetlamp. At an intersection with an alehouse, Ada heard drunks singing, off-key and slurring the lyrics, but merry all the same. She smiled at their revelry. Although she didn't exactly approve of this trip, it was exciting, and maybe no harm would come of it if they were careful.

"So where exactly are we going?" she asked.

"Viscount Manderville holds a gambling night once a week. It's not exactly respectable, but not exactly disreputable either. The masked dress-code means that men are just as likely to bring their mistresses as their wives. Although not debutants," said Mr. Ashbourne, having the grace to sound slightly ashamed, "I wouldn't take you or Hetty there, but anywhere else I could take you would be even worse. Just stay close to me and be weary of men acting too familiar. I'm sorry, I wish..." he trailed off and Ada found herself feeling bad for them. Him and Hetty really were in an impossible position.

"Oh Horatio, you mustn't worry about Ada and me," said Hetty with feeling, laying her hand on his arm. Ada looked away, uncomfortable at being party to their easy familiarity. "Ada is entirely sensible and won't do anything to compromise our reputations and I'll have the two people I trust most in the world looking out for me, so I'm sure to be fine!"

The Viscount Manderville's London townhouse was well lit but gave no other sign that a slightly dubious gambling party was taking place within its doors. Carriages pulled up surreptitiously, departed their masked passengers and drove off the same way they came. No one stood idling around the entrance exchanging light gossip like at other events, instead guests were ushered inside quickly by efficient staff. This already made it different to any event Ada had attended before.

The lack of anything remarkable outside was more than made up for by the glittering opulence that confronted Ada as a servant steered her through to what would normally be a large ballroom. Red carpet, so soft that Ada's slippers sank into it, had been laid across the floor and light from a thousand candles dazzled viewers coming in from the dark as it bounced across silver plates and crystal glasses to create rainbows of colour.

The room was dominated by a large hazard table in the centre, around which masked men and women threw both dice and money down at regular intervals. Smaller whist games were played around the edges of the room, and gentlemen in silk-brocade capes and women glittering in diamonds wandered between the tables, pausing to watch games that caught their interest and sometimes sitting down to play a set themselves.

"Oh, look, that game of whist is just coming to an end. Let us join," said Hetty, tugging Mr. Ashbourne in the direction of the table she'd spotted.

Ada turned to follow them when a strong hand gripped her elbow and she looked up to see the Duke of Aberlay, clearly recognisable despite his mask, a furious expression on his face. His eyes, which she'd thought so handsome, glittered in anger and a shot of fear went through her. He might have been kind to her before, but he was still a powerful Duke.

"Who brought you here?" he demanded.

Ada couldn't speak. He was standing so close to her that when she inhaled, the masculine scent of him filled her nostrils. She could feel the heat radiating off his body, and with it came a shiver of some deeper feeling.

"Ada?" the Duke prompted again. Any hope that he'd mistaken her for someone else evaporated.

"You recognised me."

"Answer the question," he retorted.

"I have come to act as chaperone for my sister and Mr. Ashbourne. Is my disguise so easily seen through?" she asked.

He calmed somewhat, his grip slackening. "No one else is likely to recognise you. The mask performs its task of hiding your face admirably. Nonetheless, you shouldn't be here, not even as a chaperone for your sister. It is not appropriate. Let me take you both home."

"I'm staying," said Ada. She wouldn't leave without Hetty, and she knew Hetty wouldn't leave so soon.

The Duke sighed, "I suppose you won't come to much harm if I am with you."

"You needn't nanny me the whole evening. You are free to continue doing whatever it is you were before I arrived. I shall be fine with Mr. Ashbourne and my sister," she said.

"Mr. Ashbourne and your sister have already left your side without so much as a backward glance, leaving you, an innocent, quite alone in this den of moral iniquity. There are already men looking your way with dishonourable intentions, thinking of how they will defile you, and you want me to leave you alone? My presence is the only thing stopping them from propositioning you."

Ada looked around in dismay for Mr. Ashbourne and Hetty. She finally spotted them, sitting at a whist table halfway across the room, too far away to call for if needed. She could see that what the Duke said was true. More than one man was looking at her with interest, their gazes raking shamelessly over her figure.

"With your hair loose around your face, and your bare hands, you look like a woman open to being propositioned," he said, reaching out to brush an errant tendril away from her brow. His hand trailed down her neck and slid under her domino, "I would wager you aren't wearing a corset either." His other hand slipped around her waist, fingertips tracing the thinly covered underside of her breast. Ada's heart pounded furiously in her chest. Something she'd never felt before curled tight and hot low in her stomach.

"Your Grace – "

"I told you to call me Kit," he said, so close to her that she had to tilt her head up to look him in the eye. She was keenly conscious of the scant inches between their lips.

"Kit," she breathed, her voice breaking on the single syllable.

His eyes swept down to her lips and Ada felt them part involuntarily. He was so devastatingly handsome, and Ada, stupidly, had thought herself immune because he was so far above her station. But now, surrounded by his presence, there was no denying her hopeless attraction. And with him so close, it was hard to care about differences in social status or wealth no matter how much her mind repeatedly told her the Duke would never be hers.

"If they think that you are mine, they won't dare approach you. You'll have to act as my mistress tonight," he said and then he closed the distance between them and brushed his lips possessively against hers.

Ada startled. It was the most fleeting of contact, a brief press of Kit's mouth and then gone, but not before it sent a shockwave of pleasure travelling from her lips to the very tip of her toes. It reverberated through her body, long after Kit pulled away.

"It's part of the act. Try not to look so startled. If you were my mistress, you'd be used to my kisses."

Ada blushed furiously. The thought of being familiar with Kit's kisses filled her with a desperate longing, even as it embarrassed her. What sort of woman would be able to command such regular and amorous attention from the Duke? Someone far more worldly and sophisticated than her, that much was certain.

"Come, let us take a turn about the room," he said, reaching for her hand. Ada hadn't had time for gloves. As his bare hands closed around hers, entwining their fingers together, her skin tingled at the contact and she understood why gently-bred ladies protected their hands with fabric.

They wandered between the whist tables and ever so often Kit would bring their entwined hands up to his lips to brush kisses against her fingers. Ada felt her heart might jump out of her body. This time when she looked around the room, men's eyes slid carefully away from her. Despite his mask, it was obvious who Kit was. Unlike Ada's, his was more for show, barely covering the skin around his eyes, leaving most of his face visible, including that distinctive, aristocratic nose. He hadn't even bothered taking off the large signet ring that proudly declared him an Aberlay. The hard metal of it rubbed across Ada's inner fingers on the hand the Duke refused to relinquish. A reminder of his power and status, the reason why other men didn't cross him.

But while the men no longer looked at them, the women were another matter. They eyed Kit shamelessly, coquettish eyes glancing invitingly at the Duke, making it clear he was welcome to their company whenever he wished. A hot wave of jealousy stuck in her throat and made it difficult to swallow. Unlike Ada, who hadn't had time to comb her hair or dress properly, these women were glamour and sensuality personified, their ruby red lips pouting and laughing in equal measure beneath masks that barely hid their faces. They moved with a carnal knowledge foreign to Ada that she could recognise but didn't understand. She wondered with a sickening sensation if the Duke would go home with one of these women. Or perhaps, like so many men of the ton, he kept a mistress that he'd return to at the end of the night. One who was used to his kisses in the way Ada wasn't.

"Care to try your hand at a game of hazard?" asked Kit, his eyes glinting mischievously. Ada suppressed her emotions with difficulty. She had no claim to the Duke and therefore no right to feel upset if he dallied with other women.

"I don't know how to play."

"That is no matter. I'll provide the knowledge of the gameplay if you will provide the luck," he said, leading her to the centre of the room.

Ada tried to ignore the covetous eyes that followed them but it got harder the closer they got to the hazard game. Clustered around the central table were the most daring and glamorous of the guests. There were women in near transparent dresses, some with skirts cut scandalously short to expose the calves of their legs. She was not completely naïve, she knew of the demi-monde, women who entertained rich men outside marriage, but as a well-bred lady she'd never had occasion to come into contact with any of them. Some she thought she recognised from the gossip sheets, like the famed opera singer, Lucia Vestriz, rumoured to be looking for a new patron and the notorious Harriette Wilson who reportedly was the lover of the Earl of Craven and didn't look opposed to adding the Duke of Aberlay to her conquests.

She understood now why men took mistresses. With their glamour, sexual experience and easy confidence in their bodies, these women were nothing like the ladies of the ton with their stiff posture and rigid adherence to societal rules. They were fun and playful and they encouraged male attention with their easy manners. They kissed their paramours in full public view and Ada blushed even as she watched them, wide-eyed and breathless. Unlike Kit's perfunctory press, these kisses were racy and titillating, designed to arouse with heated lips and quick flashes of tongue. So this was how people kissed when they desired each other, thought Ada. The Duke hadn't kissed her like that.

"Call the number Ada. Between two and twelve."

"Eight," she said, suddenly breathless.

Kit held the dice up to her lips and she kissed them the way she'd seen the women around the table do for the men they accompanied. Her lips brushed against the cold surface of the dice and the warm skin of Kit's fingertips. Looking up she found the Duke's dark gaze fixed unerringly on her mouth.

"Your roll," prompted the croupier.

Without looking away from Ada, Kit tossed the dice twice in his palm and flung them across the table top in a confident motion. She was distantly aware of the hush that surrounded the table, and she wondered belatedly just how much money the Duke had wagered.

"Eight!" called the croupier.

The people around them burst into chatter, but Ada's attention was solely on the Duke.

"I think a celebratory kiss is in order. You'd be remiss in your duties if you failed to congratulate me," he spoke gently against her mouth.

His eyes were gentle, questioning. Ada knew that he wouldn't insist. If she turned away from him or even ducked her head shyly that would be the end of the matter. But she didn't want to. She wanted to kiss him the way the demi-monde kissed, with teeth and tongue and more passion than sense.

She knew these weren't the thoughts of a gently-bred lady. But tonight she was supposed to be the opposite. A worldly courtesan, sensual and experienced enough to catch a Duke's attention. Keeping her gaze locked on his, Ada raised her fingertips to his jaw. He followed her lead easily, ducking his head so she could reach his lips, pausing just as they were about to touch.

Emboldened, it was Ada who closed the distance between them, pressing up and into the heat of his mouth, slanting her parted lips against his. The Duke froze, and for a moment Ada thought she'd made a mistake. But then he took control of the kiss, drawing her closer by the nape of her neck, dragging their lips together in a firm, devastating slide. Every nerve ending in Ada's body lit on fire as she melted incrementally into him.

Unlike the fleeting contact of before, this kiss was slow and thorough, the Duke making a study of her. Each press of his lips created a trembling response as she did her best to mimic his movements. The still rational part of her brain was aware that this was tame compared to the carrying on of the couples surrounding them, but this unwavering, deliberate exploration felt more wicked than anything she'd witnessed so far.

The Duke made no move to do anything more than this steady, closed-mouth kiss, and yet it was more than enough to drive Ada mad. Her pulse beat a staccato rhythm through her veins and she could feel her face and neck flushing as her body heated from his ministrations.

"Your winnings, my Lord," said a meek voice beside them.

Kit pulled back and Ada flushed in embarrassment. A servant handed over a bulging purse, then quickly fled, discreet as all the servants were. But that interruption was enough to destroy the bubble of intimacy between them.

Though a slight movement, it was unmistakable when the Duke pulled away. A rigidity in his body and a lack of expression in his face signalled a return to proper relations. Ada felt the loss keenly but also a part of her was glad nothing further had happened between them. Although it felt momentous, a closed mouth kiss was not so scandalous that Adeline would feel she'd cheated her future husband regarding her virtue.

Ada knew that courting couples sometimes exchanged chaste kisses before marriage, and sometimes the courting was a failure and both would go on to marry other people. As long as discretion was employed, society turned a blind eye, even if it wasn't strictly proper. Ada told herself that what she and the Duke had exchanged was no different. A chaste, discrete kiss, similar to those which occurred occasionally in a failed courtship. No matter that the kiss had felt positively indecent. Ada blushed all over again remembering the firm slide of Kit's lips against hers.

To distract herself, she cast about the room for Hetty and Mr. Ashbourne. That was, after all, her purpose in being here. To keep an eye on the unhappy couple and make sure nothing untoward happened, not to risk compromising herself with the darkly handsome Duke standing beside her.

And besides, at least Mr. Ashbourne wished to marry Hetty. The Duke would never stoop to wed Ada.

She spotted them closer than expected. Mr. Ashbourne was kissing Hetty's open palm with a look of such adoration that Ada's heart clenched in response. His love for her positively shone from his eyes, and Hetty was looking back at him just as tenderly. In all her years of knowing her sister, she'd never seen such affection from her before.

"They really do love each other," said Ada. Any hope that it might be a passing infatuation faded as she watched them.

The Duke followed her gaze.

"My parents," continued Ada, "especially Mama, had hoped for a far better match for Hetty. They will never accept this."

"What could be a better match than a gentleman of honour who loves your sister and can claim her love in return," said the Duke.

"I would've thought you of all people would disapprove. You hold the highest title in the land. Your entire family is wealthy and highly connected. You cannot tell me you do not know the importance of a woman marrying well."

"There are things far more precious in this world than wealth and social status. Your sister might marry a title and have more money as a result, but will it make up for losing the man she loves forever? I doubt it."

Ada pondered this. Her sister moved through life with a certain careless joy that made it difficult to believe her capable of being seriously hurt. But the depth and duration of her feelings had been something Ada would never have anticipated. After all, Hetty remained consistent in her affection for Mr Ashbourne for over a year. That sounded like neither a whim nor a fancy but rather spoke of a deep and lasting devotion that until now Ada had believed her sister incapable of. The last thing she wanted was to see her sister in pain, her joy for life and carefree nature damaged by the loss of love. If Mr Ashbourne was the one person in the world that Hetty cared for above all others, then Ada wouldn't be much of a sister if she didn't support her.

She sighed. "At least they can live on her dowry. Since Mr Ashbourne doesn't have a penny to his name."

"That's not quite true. He has two thousand a year from his mother and a commission in the army. It is not enough to live extravagantly I'll admit, but they certainly will not starve, even if your sister wed him without any money of her own."

This was news to Ada, and it made things not quite so hopeless for Hetty. Two thousand a year was only a little less than what her father had when mother married him. And Ada and Hetty would get twenty thousand a piece as dowry when they wed and another ten thousand each when Mama passed. Like the Duke said, it was not extravagant, but they wouldn't starve. In fact, if it wasn't for the fact that Mama expected so much for Hetty, it would be a very suitable match. Hetty would be marrying neither above nor beneath the station she was born in.

"There is also every possibility that Ashbourne will distinguish himself in military service. And he might win himself a handsome fortune as a result, perhaps even gain the title your mother craves so much."

"I wish for Hetty's sake that it would happen as you say. I agree that there is nothing wrong with the match and everything to like especially since it would ensure my sister's happiness. But I doubt Mama will see it that way, and Papa is not likely to give permission for the match if Mama disapproves."

The Duke's brow furrowed and Ada had a sudden urge to wipe away his frown with a press of her fingers. She buried the urge deep and for extra security folded her hands behind her back. Every woman in the ton knew that the Duke was incredibly handsome, it was natural that Ada would react to that. But she refused to behave like the simpering debutants that hounded him for attention.

"Let me talk to your father," said the Duke.

Ada's mouth fell open in surprise. She quickly shut it, but the shock remained. "You would do that for Hetty?"

The Duke looked at her for a long moment, and at last said, "For your sister, yes."

It was said with such solemn intensity that for a moment Adeline thought the Duke might have feelings for Hetty after all. A wave of jealousy and sadness bubbled up to the surface, ugly and unwanted. Years of being compared to her sister, being told her sister was the beauty and Ada the ugly one had never hurt as much as in this moment. Perhaps if Ada had been blessed with as much beauty as Hetty, the Duke might just possibly have considered courting Ada.

She dismissed the entire thought as foolish. Even Hetty's beauty wasn't likely to tempt the Duke, who had access to the most beautiful women of the ton, many of whom Ada could admit were Hetty's equal in looks if viewed from an objective lens. Besides, the Duke would hardly offer to advocate for another man's suit if he held any designs for Hetty. No, he was just honourable and kind and disposed to help. And Ada was getting stupidly emotionally entangled with a man who would never feel anything for her.

Chapter 7
A Woman's Honour

Both Ada and Hetty were trying and failing to stifle yawns at breakfast the next morning. It felt like they'd barely slept before it was time to wake up. All Ada wanted was to return to bed, but then Mama would want to know why and if she feigned sickness, she wouldn't be able to attend Almack's tonight and it was vitally important that she did.

Ada had failed in her role as chaperone, and now it was up to her to fix it. Last night, after an hour or so in the Duke's company, he'd returned her to Hetty. Ada had been so preoccupied by her own affairs that evening, she'd failed to notice the changes in her sister. The high colour of her cheeks, her hair messier than before, the missed button on her dress. It was only when they were safely in their room again that the truth came pouring out of Hetty and Ada had listened with an increasing sense of shock and horror.

"We got carried away. Mr. Ashbourne and I," Hetty had said, even her liveliness fading as the magnitude of her actions sunk in.

"What do you mean? Did you exchange a kiss?" asked Ada, still thinking of her own kiss with the Duke and not comprehending the depth of peril her sister was in.

"We went further than a kiss."

It was the expression on Hetty's face that first clued Ada in. Her sister was pale, hands trembling slightly.

"How much further?" she'd asked, desperately hoping the answer wasn't what she feared.

"I am technically what they call a ruined woman," said Hetty, with a nervous laugh.

"Oh Hetty. How could you? What possessed you?"

Hetty sat down heavily on her bed. "When you love someone and want to be with them desperately, it's the easiest thing in the world. It is denying yourself that is difficult. And after over a year of it, our self-control was shaky at best. If Mama and Papa had just listened to what I wanted last year, all of this could have been prevented."

"So this is some kind of revenge on them?"

"No, of course not! What kind of revenge is it anyway if it hurts you more than the people you seek retribution from," Hetty had said.

"It hurt? Ashbourne hurt you?" asked Ada.

"Never. He would never hurt me. I meant the emotional pain of your love being something to feel guilty for, to feel ashamed about. I pray you never experience it, Ada. It is over now at least, thank the Lord. I confess I feel some relief that matters have come to a head."

"Yes, you will have to marry. There is no other choice."

"It is a choice I have ever wanted to make."

The earnestness of her sister's reply sent a pang through Ada's heart. "Oh Hetty, I will be sad to see you go. And sad that it happened in these circumstances. But if this is what you need to ensure your happiness, then I will be happy for you also."

"You always were the best of sisters. Thank you Ada. It is likely I shall need your help before this is all over."

"You have it," said Ada firmly, sitting beside Hetty and taking her hand.

"We'll go to Gretna Green at the nearest opportunity. Horatio thinks he'll be able to get horses and lodgings sorted in three days, four at the most."

"Why? You don't need to elope Hetty. If you tell Mama and Papa what happened, they will sanction the match. They won't have any other choice."

"I can't do it Ada. I can't face their wrath. Mama's anger. She will be furious."

"Let her be furious. There is nothing they can do to you anyway. Our dowry is from our grandfather. And Mama's marriage contract stipulates her wealth must be split evenly between any remaining heirs. So your inheritance is safe also."

Hetty shook her head. "I am not like you Ada. You've always been able to take Mama's harshness and remain unaffected. I am not strong enough."

Ada had taken her mother's insults in stride because she didn't have any choice, not because she possessed any unique strength.

"Hetty, think of what elopement means. A hasty marriage can be rationalised. A wedding in Gretna Green will never be anything less than a scandal."

"What shall I care for scandal when I am wed? Horatio and I will disappear to the continent where I shall be a military wife and live in happiness. Wagging tongues won't reach us there."

They might not reach Hetty, but Ada, stuck here in London, would not fare so well. A better-connected family might weather the storm, but the smallest whiff of scandal surrounding Ada would see invitations dry up. For the mere daughter of a country baronet, the elopement of a sister would mean social disaster. She tried a different angle.

"Surely Mr Ashbourne must see the perils of elopement. His brother, Lord Beulle, will be anxious to avoid a scandal. And the Duke of Aberlay assured me he would be willing to speak to Papa on your behalf. You are not without friends Hetty, let us help you resolve this."

"That is true. Sarah, Horatio's sister by marriage, has assured me repeatedly that both she and Lord Beulle are anxious for our happiness. I am sure they would prefer a regular marriage. But the scandal will not affect them over much. No one will dare snub a Viscount's family because of his brother's elopement. Sarah and Lord Buelle are very established in society."

Ada had been reluctant to bring up her own concerns. The last thing she'd wanted was to be selfish in the face of Hetty's troubles, but it was likely that her sister who often lived in a world of her own hadn't considered all the implications. "I agree that the Viscount's family is likely to be unaffected. But our family won't be as fortunate. Papa and Mama won't enjoy the same social reception they do now with a daughter recently eloped." And neither will I, she'd added mentally in her head.

"Oh. I hadn't thought of that," said her sister, "How awful." That was typical for Hetty. Her breezy self-involvement was part of her charm.

"Will you consider then, telling our parents the truth of why you and Ashbourne must wed?"

Hetty looked distressed, "If I must, I suppose, but Ada, I would so much rather not. Surely there is some other way this can be arranged."

Ada thought a moment. "If His Grace, the Duke of Aberlay, and the Viscount Buelle bring Ashbourne's suit to father, it will be difficult for him to say no. Hopefully there will be no need to mention, well, you know..." she trailed off awkwardly.

"Me being ruined?" asked Hetty with a giggle.

"Yes, exactly," said Ada.

"Funny how I can do it so easily, and yet talking about it is absurd."

"It was easy?"

"The easiest, most natural thing in the world. Oh Ada, I know I should be ashamed of it, but in truth, it was wonderful. The most beautiful thing I've ever experienced."

Ada had fallen asleep with rather scandalous ideas swirling in her mind, along with a far greater understanding of the mechanics of carnal knowledge than was proper for a debutante to know. Some of the things Hetty had mentioned sounded disgusting and uncomfortable, but her sister had acted like it was all quite the opposite.

"Are you girls listening? The Duchess of Aberlay!" The Duke's title in her mother's shrill voice rudely interrupted Ada's musings, bringing her attention sharply back to the breakfast table.

"What about the Duke?" asked Ada.

Hetty shot her a glance which she ignored.

"Her Grace, the Duchess of Aberlay has invited us to one of her exclusive soirees. A picnic at her house. Really, I thought you girls would be more excited. Hetty must have caught the Duke's eye. What other explanation can there be for being included all of a sudden," said Mama with a dreamy expression on her face.

Ada snatched the invitation from her mother's grasp. It was a sign of Mama's happiness that her behaviour went unremarked.

"A women's picnic lunch," said Ada reading from the invitation, "It doesn't sound like the Duke will be there."

"Well, no, but his mother and sister will," said Mama, taking the invitation back, "and their good opinion will be important to the Duke. And if the Dowager Duchess truly takes a shine to Hetty, just think what that would do to our prospects. Why, Her Grace is a patroness of Almack's. Speaking of which, you girls need to be getting ready soon. Did you sleep poorly, Hetty? You look tired."

Luckily Mama required no reply, she continued on as if one had been given.

"Well never mind, we'll get a cold press under your eyes and some rouge on your cheeks and that'll perk you right up." She looked at Ada with a frown. "Same treatment for both of you I think. Ada you look even worse than usual."

For Almack's the dresses were once again the work of Madam Jacqueline. These had been delivered earlier as part of both her and Hetty's wardrobe for the new season. Just like at the Queen's ball, Ada marvelled at the quality of the fabric and trims. Hetty's gown, which was finer than Ada's, even had a bit of lace on the panelling, a tremendous expense that made her garment look as fine as anything an heiress might wear. Ada knew both her parents had diligently saved their income so their daughters could have London seasons, and she was grateful to them for it.

Not all parents showed such foresight. Miss Maria Conley back in Riverstoke was, in Ada's quiet opinion, just as handsome as Hetty, and her family estate generated a similar amount to Papa's. If Maria's father had shown some economy, he could likely have managed the expense of sending his daughter to London, especially since he only had one. But the

Conley's spent lavishly, though it was true that Mrs Conley was not so high-born as Mama.

Although Mama was harsh on her and quarrelsome, Ada was aware that without her impetus neither she nor Hetty would be here, firmly entrenched in the London Season. It was Mama who'd arranged the governesses for their education, ensured her daughters' manners and dress would allow them to blend seamlessly into the ton, and it was her connections as the daughter of a Baron and the sister to a Countess and Baroness that had secured them an invitation to the exclusive Almack's.

Was it any wonder then that Mama was anxious Hetty marry well. The time, attention and money she invested in her daughters far exceeded that of any other family Ada knew in their village. And the generous dowry Lord Hayne had bequeathed to each of his granddaughters at birth, meant that she and Hetty could, at least in financial terms, be considered suitable spouses for most men of the ton.

Though Mama had income from her own dowry, she must always be keenly aware of the difference in means between her life now, and the life she had enjoyed as the daughter of a wealthy Baron. Was it any wonder she wanted better for her daughters? Or at least better for Hetty, who was the only one likely to catch the eye of a superior match. And even if Ada couldn't marry as well, Mama would be aware that Ada's social position would be elevated by her sister's.

Mama had no notion of it yet, but all her plans and hopes for Hetty had faded to dust. Mr Ashbourne was a respectable choice, but not a dazzling one. Not the kind of choice that would thrust their family into the pinnacle of society. Ada agreed with the Duke that the love Ashbourne and Hetty felt for each other meant the wedding between them shouldn't be prevented, especially in light of recent events. But still, she could not help feel sorry for Mama, who would find this match a bitter reward for her work.

"Ada! Try not to slouch so," said Mama, coming for a final check before Almack's, "Honestly, even if you won't be a great beauty, you can at least conduct yourself in a ladylike fashion. Hetty dear, lovely as always."

The earlier sympathy Ada had felt evaporated. She tried not to roll her eyes. It would only risk another reprimand anyway.

"Into the carriage with both of you. Quickly now. They won't let us in if we're late!"

Ada's first impression of Almack's was rather underwhelming. After the grandeur of Queen Charlotte's debutante ball, perhaps any place would look dull. But the series of plain-walled rooms that served as the venue for London's most exclusive social club seemed to Ada particularly uninspiring.

The people though were as impressive as before. Ladies dressed in the finest silks and draped head to toe with jewels. Gentlemen all in smart breeches and well-tailored coats to show off their athletic physiques, or in some cases, not-so-athletic physiques. Perhaps that was the true wonder of Almack's, not the venue, but the fact that all of London's most exclusive citizens congregated here.

She scanned the room slowly, taking in its occupants. There was Lady Jersey holding court amongst a group of gentlemen. And Lady Selina, last season's most celebrated debutante, now the Countess of Stanhope. Supposedly the Earl had fallen head over heels. There was Ashbourne, eagerly scanning the entrance. His face breaking into an expression of such joy when he saw Hetty that Ada's heart gave a sympathetic pang.

Mama was less impressed. "I wish that Mr. Ashbourne would keep away. What is he even doing here?"

"He is the son and brother of a Viscount," said Ada, "And he has two thousand a year. Even you must admit Mama, those are strong credentials for admittance to Almack's."

Her mother was prevented from replying by the man's arrival. Which was just as well, since her sour expression indicated it would be nothing good.

"Lady Duefont, Miss Duefont, Miss Adeline Duefont," greeted Mr. Ashbourne. His manners were almost perfect, except for the fact he looked exclusively at Hetty, "Miss Duefont, may I have the honour of this dance?"

Mama looked like she'd swallowed a lemon. She opened her mouth, but Hetty got there first.

"I'd be delighted," she exclaimed, leaving with him immediately.

"Hetty couldn't have turned him down anyway," said Ada consolingly to Mama, "We've only just arrived so it's obvious our dance cards are empty. And if she feigned illness, we'd have to leave."

"It's a waste of a dance. And the first dance too," said Mama, "someone far better could come along at any moment and there is Hetty dancing with a second son who'll never inherit anything. Why, the Duke of Aberlay is right there!"

Ada's head snapped around, and sure enough there he was, aloof and regal as ever. She hadn't noticed him in her initial scan, standing as he was, a little behind them and in an alcove. The Viscount Manderville stood with him and together they were a sight that drew more than a few female glances. Both tall, of similar build and very handsome. But it was the Duke that held Ada's attention.

That wave of stark black hair, his piercing eyes, lips that looked stern, but as Ada knew from last night, would feel unbearably soft against hers. She flushed at the remembrance. As if sensing the scrutiny, Kit turned his head. A shock went through her as their eyes met. He raised an eyebrow as if asking a question. Feeling bashful, Ada ducked her head and returned a shy smile.

The Duke said something to his companion and then he was striding towards her. His footsteps eating up the floor space between them. Even the way he walked was attractive. Confident, self-assured. How much of that was inherently Kit and how much due to his position Ada didn't know. Despite Almack's being filled with Lords and Ladies, powerful individuals alike in social status and rank, it was obvious that the Duke sat a level above. Heads turned as he walked, women tittered, and men nodded their respects. A few tried to intercept him, but he deftly avoided them, his eyes fixed on Ada. She would be lying if she claimed that the focused attention of such a man was not incredibly flattering.

Mama audibly gasped. "The Duke is coming our way. Didn't I just say that going with Mr. Ashbourne was a blunder. To think Hetty might have danced with the Duke. And now she's missed her chance. This is too horrible."

"Lady Duefont. Miss Adeline Duefont. Will you dance with me?" He said, hand outstretched, a smile playing on his lips. That hand had held her when they'd kissed last night. There was no world in which she said no.

"I was hoping to talk to you tonight," she said as he led her away.

"And I you."

He was being polite, but it pleased her all the same. "It's about last night."

"Oh. Is there something from last night you wish to revisit?" he asked, his voice dropping lower.

Ada flushed. "It is to do with Hetty. Hetty and Ashbourne. Did you mean what you said last night?"

Kit led her to the front of the set. Just like last time, Ada felt everyone looking at them. Perils of dancing with a Duke. "That they should marry. Yes, I did."

Ada ignored the familiar thrill of Kit's arms encircling her. It wouldn't do to get distracted by him again. She'd already made that mistake last night.

"I meant what you said about speaking for them. It is a lot to ask. But, well, I think it would help them." Perhaps the Duke had only been courteous and didn't really mean his offer of assistance, and now Ada was putting him in a tight spot by bringing it up.

"I meant what I said. I'm ready to go to your father this instant."

Ada's lips twitched. "Not right this instant perhaps. People will think I've offended you badly if you leave in the middle of the dance."

Kit smiled. "There's nothing you could say that would offend me."

"No? Even if I did or said something scandalous?"

He raised an eyebrow at this. "On the contrary I'd enjoy it. Besides, what could you possibly say that would be so shocking?" His voice dropped lower. "I kissed you last night, I know what an innocent you are."

Ada blushed, but some wild urge overtook her, and she looked at him boldly, refusing to cower, her own voice dropping in response. "I could tell you how much I liked it. How your mouth against mine was the best thing I've ever felt."

The Duke's eyes widened, but before he could respond, the dance required them to switch partners. Kit looked frustrated as he handed her over to the gentleman in the couple beside them and took the lady into his own arms.

Ada placed her hand in the gentleman's palm and noted it was slightly sweaty. He was shorter than Kit too, closer to her own height, with ash-brown hair and a slightly pudgy face. She took all this in, even as her mind spun with her behaviour. For all their joking, what she'd said had been shocking. She should have kept quiet. It was as if when she talked to the Duke, a little imp sat under her tongue and bade her to challenge and tease him at every turn, no matter how improper.

"I do not think we've been introduced," the man before her said, a bright smile on his face.

"Adeline Duefont," she said.

"Lawrence Mellford. It's a pleasure to meet the most beautiful woman in the room."

Ada laughed, "And I can see *I've* met the greatest flatterer in the room."

He spun her and Ada felt it odd how his flowery compliment produced not even the slightest thrill in her. She felt only mild amusement, whereas a single word from Kit sent her heart whizzing about like a bee caught in a jar. Perhaps when a girl had kissed a Duke, there was little else that could rattle her.

"I assure you, I am normally terrible at giving compliments. I once told my aunt she looked good for her age. She was offended for a week."

"That's an amateur mistake. Women want to be told they don't look a day over twenty."

"Well then Miss Duefont, you don't look a day over twenty."

Ada laughed again, "That would've worked except that I'm younger than twenty. So now you've aged me as well as your aunt."

Mr. Mellford grinned and shook his head at himself. "See. Terrible at giving compliments."

"You're better than most I've met."

"I fear I need to hand you over in a second. But will you do me the honour of dancing the next set? That is if your card is free."

"I'd be delighted."

The Duke's hand closed over hers and any thought of Mr. Mellford or anyone else flew from her mind as swiftly as a deer from a wolf. She looked up, far further than her last partner, and that same bolt of electricity shot through her as their eyes met. His piercing gaze seemed to look past her very skin and into the squishy, inner part of her where emotions were stored.

"It seems you were luckier in your dance partner than me," he said mildly.

"Oh no. Did you get another simpering one?"

The Duke nodded with such an exaggerated grimace that Ada had to laugh.

"It is no laughing matter! I'm hounded by these women."

"I'm sorry, I'll try and be more sympathetic," said Ada, "Poor Kit, it must be so difficult to be obscenely rich and shockingly handsome, and a Duke besides. How terrible for you to have all the most beautiful women of the ton throwing themselves at your feet."

That drew a smile out of him. "You think I'm handsome."

Oh no, Ada hadn't meant to give that away. It was bad enough having a slight infatuation for the Duke, she'd die if he found out about it. "Well, I'm not blind. Your features are aesthetically pleasing." She slid her eyes away from his, feeling her face flush. "Anyway, I wanted to talk to you about Hetty and Ashbourne. And the dance is almost over."

Kit spun her a little closer and Ada tried not to be affected by it. "I recall. You want me to petition your father about it. And I'm happy to do so."

"Can you do it tonight?"

"Tonight?" he said, "That soon? I suppose. But it would be prudent to bring Viscount Buelle into it as well. It is his brother after all. Is there any reason to rush?"

Ada bit her lip pensively. Kit's eyes dropped to her mouth and Ada pretended she didn't find it distracting. Ideally, she would keep Hetty's secret. But they needed the Duke to bring all his power and influence to bear on Papa.

"Hetty and Ashbourne are planning to elope." That was half of it, and hopefully serious enough a statement to warrant Kit's cooperation.

He frowned. "They mustn't. It would be an unnecessary scandal. Can you not convince your sister to wait? I am confident I can get your father to agree to the match given enough time."

"I cannot. And I will not. Kit, promise me you won't breathe a word to anyone of this," she said. He nodded his agreement and Ada let out a shaky breath. "They must be married with all haste. There is no other choice. Elopement would be preferable even to a long engagement because, well, last night, they did something…" she trailed off, her face turning bright hot.

There was understanding in the Duke's expression which Ada was grateful for. "Say no more. I understand completely."

"I am so worried. My sister, she's on the cusp of ruin, and I'm helpless to do anything about it. It's my fault, I should have stuck closely to her last night. Hetty's not good at thinking of consequences, as a child I was always the practical one, and now, when I should have been there for her, I wasn't." Ada blinked rapidly, willing away a glaze of tears. The last thing she needed was to be known as the girl who cried at Almack's.

The dance ended and instead of releasing her, the Duke held on more tightly, "Please darling, do not distress yourself. I promise you, I will fix this. Hetty and Ashbourne will be married with haste, even if I have to drag the respective parties down the aisle myself."

The endearment shocked Ada out of her worry. *Darling.* Had the Duke really called her that?

"Miss Duefont, I've come to claim the next dance," said a loud voice beside them.

"Ah, Mr Mellford, give me a moment to grab a refreshment," said Ada, needing a respite. The Duke released her and she felt the loss keenly. Mr Mellford didn't have the same effect at all.

"Let me fetch one for you."

"No, that's quite alright," she called back, already heading towards the drinks table. Across a white cloth sat rows of pink and yellow lemonade. Not a lot of choice. Ada settled on yellow, taking a sip from her glass and trying not to wince at the taste. A woman sidled up to her casually, inspecting the selection. Ada turned and her eyes widened in surprise. The Dowager Duchess of Aberlay, patroness of Almack's, quite possibly the most powerful woman in society. Her daughter was the Marchioness of Reeth, and her son, Ada swallowed, her son was the Duke.

"How do you find the refreshments at Almack's?" asked the Dowager Duchess.

Ada tried to quieten her nerves. "If I was being polite, which I believe is a requirement for entry, I would say they are delicious and invigorating."

"And if not being polite?"

"They taste like someone added sugar to bathwater."

To Ada's surprise the Dowager Duchess gave a loud laugh. Several heads turned in their direction. "I should probably disapprove of that statement. But it is too accurate. You've captured it exactly," said the Duchess, "Anyway it is I who have been impolite. I never introduced myself."

"That is hardly necessary, Your Grace, everyone knows you. But I am nowhere near as famous, so allow me to introduce myself."

"Equally unnecessary Miss Adeline Duefont," said the older woman with a twinkle in her eye, "Perhaps you are more famous than you think."

"That seems unlikely. I haven't done anything of note."

"No? Two dances with an unmarried Duke in a matter of days. Most of the ton find that rather noteworthy. Make it three and you'll really get them chattering."

"Kit, His Grace," Ada quickly corrected, "Is most kind."

"Kit, is it?" said the Duchess, not only noticing her slip, but drawing attention to it. Ada wished she could sink through the ground. "I would love to talk further, but that gentleman seems quite anxious for your attention. Anyway, I suspect we shall be seeing quite a lot of each other in the future."

Not knowing if the Duchess meant that kindly or as a threat, Ada only nodded before scurrying over to Mr Mellford.

"Apologies. I got caught in a conversation."

"No apology necessary!" said Mr Mellford, "I wouldn't fob off the Dowager Duchess of Aberlay either. My mother had a conversation with her once and she brings it up constantly, at every country ball. The time the famous Duchess talked to her."

"I'm sure the villagers are very impressed by that," said Ada absentmindedly. She was only half-concentrating on Mellford. Most of her thoughts were turned towards her sister. As a Duke, Kit had a level of power and influence difficult for Ada to comprehend. But she also knew from stern talks with Mama and governesses that Hetty was in the worst kind of trouble a gently-bred woman could be in. She desperately hoped this could be fixed as Kit said. Oh Hetty, Ada thought, why couldn't you have been a little more sensible?

Chapter 8
A Bride & Groom

"Adeline, wake up!"

Ada awoke to her sister shaking her. She blinked up blearily at Hetty, who seeing Ada's open eyes left her to dance about the room like some sort of mad fae spirit clad in a nightgown. She watched this bizarre spectacle for a moment, trying to make sense of it.

"What on earth is going on Hetty?"

Henrietta Duefont clapped her hands together. "Oh Ada, it's all so wonderful I can scarcely believe it. The Duke of Aberlay was here early this morning with Viscount Buelle and Horatio. I only found out when Papa called me into his study."

Ada sat up with a start. "Papa agreed to the marriage?"

Hetty grinned. "From what he told me he had little choice. I understand they positively browbeat him into it. He agreed before Mama awoke, in fact while all of us were asleep. But he has given his word now and can't take it back! They signed a contract and everything. And Viscount Buelle said he would announce it in this morning's paper. So Papa really can't back out, no matter how much Mama rails at him."

"Hetty that's wonderful," said Adeline, forgetting any lingering fatigue to sweep her sister up in a tight hug, "I'm so happy for you!"

"Oh Ada, me too," said Hetty, her voice clogged with emotion, "I never thought I could be so happy."

As she hugged her sister, Ada gave silent thanks for the Duke of Aberlay. He had kept his word. She briefly allowed herself to imagine what it would be like to have him always on her side. The reassurance and safety she would feel, wrapped in the cocoon of his protection. Then she let it go. Kit couldn't be that for her.

In a way, Hetty was the more sensible sister. She'd fallen in love with someone who returned her affection and would offer marriage. Ada startled at the path her thoughts had taken. Surely what she felt for the Duke couldn't be love? They'd met but a handful of times. And yet, weren't those encounters enough to know his character? At times he could seem so aloof, but he was always willing to laugh with her and respond to her teasing with quips of his own. And beneath the exterior, there was great kindness. He'd helped Hetty and Ashbourne when asked, without judgement or condescension. Yes, it was definitely at least the beginning tendrils of love, thought Ada with dismay, feeling as if thousands of tiny strings were tugging at her heart.

"What is it?" asked Hetty pulling away slightly.

Ada plastered a smile on her face, "I just can't believe you are going to be married. When is it happening?"

Hetty laughed. "Within days! The Duke obtained a special licence! Can you believe it? They're fabulously expensive. But I suppose money isn't really a problem for him. And I'm sure the Archbishop couldn't say no to the Duke."

"We must pay him back for any expenses he's incurred. I asked him for this favour."

"Don't be silly Ada, he's so rich he won't even notice. Besides, a few pounds for a marriage licence is nothing compared to what he's settled on Horatio."

"Hetty, what do you mean? What has the Duke settled on Mr. Ashbourne?"

"Why he's only gone and given us ten thousand pounds, and the Viscount, Horatio's brother, insisted on matching the sum. So Horatio will have twenty thousand as well as the income he inherited from his mother. Papa wasn't able to argue lack of financial support because Horatio will have the same as Papa does."

Ada ran the numbers in her head. The interest on twenty thousand would push Ashbourne's income up to match their father's, a fact that wouldn't have been lost on Kit. When Ada had asked for help, she'd assumed he'd only talk to Papa and make him see sense. This went above and beyond. It was a level of generosity difficult to comprehend. More than Ada could ever repay. Kit gave generously not only of his time and influence, but also of his riches.

"We will never be able to repay him," said Ada. The sum was too vast. Half of Ada's entire dowry, and Lord Buelle's portion would take the other half. Although at least the Viscount was Ashbourne's family and therefore hadn't acted as a particular favour to Ada or Hetty, but rather for his brother's sake.

"That's what I've been trying to tell you! It's impossible so there's no reason to bother. Anyway, Horatio already tried to offer and the Duke flat out refused. Stop worrying about it and be happy like I am! Besides, if you're going to worry about anything, it should be Mama. I've never seen her in such a rage."

Ada winced. "She knows then."

"I'm surprised her shouting didn't wake you. They probably heard it two doors over. Lucky for us the Duke and Lord Buelle had left by the time she discovered it. She was so angry she might have forgotten herself and yelled at them. Can you imagine it? As it was, Papa bore the brunt of it, although my ears are still ringing from the few times she turned her ire on me."

Hetty seemed to find the whole thing amusing, and given that she was soon to be married to the man she loved, Ada could forgive her exuberance. But this would be a huge blow to Mama.

"Where is she now?" asked Ada.

"I think she went back to bed. Said she couldn't stand to look at either of us. Oh Ada there's so much to do, so much packing and sewing to get everything ready. Where is Sarah? I must find her and begin at once."

Ada left Hetty to her preparations and walked down the corridor to Mama's room, knocking tentatively at her door.

"Leave me be," came a muffled voice.

"Mama, it's me, Ada. I'm coming in."

Mama who normally rushed everywhere with an annoying amount of energy was a sad lump on the bed, her face hidden in the pillows and her hair unkempt. Ada took a comb from the dresser and sat beside her, carefully working out the knots.

"You have heard that Hetty is to be married then?" said Mama after a long moment.

"Yes, I heard," said Ada, continuing to comb, hoping the action was soothing.

Mama turned to face her. "All my work and effort, trying to make sure you girls had an education equal to any lady of the ton, equal to your cousins, and Hetty just threw it away. Do you know how hard I've struggled to ensure you didn't suffer for my poor marriage? And now it has all come to nought."

"I know Mama," said Ada.

Her mother grabbed her arm. "Ada, marriage is the only financial choice a woman gets to make in her life. That one act determines our entire future. Whether you scrimp and save to provide your daughters with a London season or whether you attend every year like my mother and sisters, and don't even think about money because their husbands have plenty. Hetty will have to economise her whole life."

"I think that is a sacrifice Hetty is willing to make."

Mama snorted. "Hetty has no idea what she's giving up. As much as I love her, she can't see past the nose on her face. She makes all her choices in life based on feeling, not thinking of the consequences. She is not practical like you and I Ada. And God knows I tried to be practical for her."

"I know you did Mama."

Her mother sighed deeply. "I wish you had been the beautiful one Ada. You would've been more sensible about it, made the best match you could. Unfortunate that you take after me, both of us unfashionably dark."

Ada wished that too. If she were more beautiful, maybe the Duke could have loved her back. "Well, we'll have to make the most of it," said Ada, injecting false cheer into her voice, "You need to get dressed Mama, don't forget the Dowager Duchess of Aberlay's picnic is today. You were so excited about it yesterday."

"Oh, don't speak to me about the Aberlays. Haven't they meddled enough in our lives? I have no idea how Lord Buelle managed to involve the Duke in this affair, but it was underhand in the extreme. It would take a man stronger than your father to stand up to the Duke and perhaps he was right to give in. The Aberlays' disapproval would mean social suicide."

"Exactly, so we can hardly fob off the Duchess when we've been invited to her exclusive house picnic. Besides, you still have me to marry off Mama. Who knows, I might make a better match than you expect. At Almack's Mr Mellford was very attentive and I danced with Lord Petterington who is a Baron."

Mama sniffed, "An impoverished one and likely hunting for a fortune," she said, but she did sit up and Ada noticed she looked less unhappy.

"Well, what about Mellford then?"

"He has six thousand a year. Not a bad match at all," said Mama, perking up more as her matchmaking instincts kicked in. "No title of course, but who knows, his uncle could die without an heir and make Mellford a Lord."

"If you say so, Mama."

"I do say so. What are you doing still in your nightdress Ada? We have a picnic to get to! And you must seem as desirable as possible. I wonder if any of Mellford's relations will be invited."

Chapter 9
Breakfast

Kit was exhausted. He slept poorly at the best of times, and last night he hadn't even made it to his bed. Adeline's face, consumed with worry for her sister, kept him awake as readily as distant gunshots and cannon fire. When she opened up to him about her fears, something twisted in his heart and refused to let go. He needed her to be happy, more than he'd ever needed anything, and the realisation floored him. What did it mean that this delightful, beautiful, self-conscious creature had the premier spot in his thoughts and desires? Love? The word rose to Kit's thoughts unbidden. He pushed it away just as quickly. He could admit affection. To think himself in love was a step too far.

Kit took a long sip of his coffee, hoping it would fortify him. His mother sat opposite in her morning gown, looking as well rested as always and entirely too pleased with herself. She seemed to thrive in the London Season. It wasn't surprising to Kit that she didn't drink coffee. Gossip and scandal seemed to be the only fuel she needed.

"Is Marianne coming any time soon?" he asked, glancing at his pocket watch, "I need to be in Parliament in a half hour."

When the three of them were in London, they often had breakfast together, although due to his sister's tardiness, half the time it ended with Kit having breakfast with his mother and leaving before Marianne's arrival.

"Who can say," said his mother with an elegant shrug, "Marianne was late to her own wedding, we can hardly expect her to be on time for breakfast. Speaking of weddings, I bumped into the archbishop today. We had a most fascinating conversation."

The cat-like grin on her face instantly put him on guard. He wasn't going to make it any easier for her. She could plainly state whatever she wanted to needle out of him. "The archbishop is a learned man. I am sure he can speak intelligently on a variety of topics and it is therefore no surprise that a conversation with him would be, as you put it, fascinating."

"In this particular instance, it wasn't theology that interested me. You can imagine my surprise upon learning that my only son had this morning sought a special marriage licence without nary a word to me about it! Of course, a grown man is no longer answerable to his mother, but is it too much to hope that he informs his dear mama if he is soon to wed, so that she too can share in his happiness?" She accompanied all this with an unconvincing sniff.

Kit resisted the urge to roll his eyes. His mother would have extracted every last morsel of information out of the archbishop, including the information that the marriage parties were a Mr Horatio Ashbourne and a Miss Henrietta Deufont. "You know very well that I am not getting married. I assure you if I am ever to undertake the venture, you will be amongst the first to know."

"It is a relief to hear that. But you will understand my confusion when I saw that one of the parties on the marriage licence had the same last name as a certain lady you seem to keep dancing with. Deufont. I remembered it being mentioned in the gossip columns next to yours. Of course, it later dawned on me that the woman in question was the younger sister, a Miss Adeline Deufont."

His mother thought she knew something, and that made her dangerous. Kit gritted his teeth, "I danced with her twice, that's hardly a pattern."

"That's already twice as much as any other lady and now you've sought a marriage licence on her sister's behalf."

"Mother, please don't interfere," said Kit, feeling the start of a headache coming on.

"Me? Interfere in the romantic entanglements of my children? I never heard such an absurd statement. Why, I might aid and assist and nudge my wayward offspring into seeing common sense, but that is all for their benefit."

Kit snorted. Even his mother couldn't suppress a smile.

"Well, maybe I interfere a little, but with the best of intentions."

"Intentions didn't help Marianne, did it? There is little happiness to be found in her marriage."

A dark cloud passed over Mama's face. The Dowager Duchess had had high hopes for her only daughter and in terms of title and wealth, Marianne had made the best catch of the season. But in terms of happiness, the serious

Marquess of Reeth, for all his impressive titles and wealth, had proved a poor match for the carefree, fun-loving Marianne.

"Well, we aren't here to talk about Marianne's marriage," said his mother brightly, "I'm far more interested in yours."

Kit rolled his eyes, "My non-existent marriage that exists only in your head."

"You know I talked to her at Almack's, your Miss Adeline. She came across as a very forthright young lady."

Kit looked at his mother for a long moment, trying to identify the curious expression on her face, before his eyes widened incrementally, "You like her," he said with a degree of astonishment.

"Why is that so surprising?" she asked.

Kit snorted. "You're the biggest snob I know. You wouldn't hear of Marianne marrying anyone beneath an Earl and you did everything in your power to ensure she was wed to the highest-ranking bachelor at the time despite her own objections."

"A woman's marriage determines her position in society. A man's rank is entirely his own and is conferred upon his wife. You see the difference?"

He nodded in acquiescence to her point.

"A man, especially one with rank and fortune, is free to marry as he will," she continued, "His choice of spouse makes little material difference to his life except to increase or decrease his happiness. So you may as well marry to please yourself. Someone in this family ought to." There was the smallest hint of bitterness in her voice that he only picked up on because he knew her so well.

"It seems unfair," said Kit.

His mother smiled wryly. "You needn't feel too sorry for your sister or I. There are far worse fates in this world than being a Duchess or a Marchioness. Your father and I respected each other. And Lord Reeth is an honourable man, he treats your sister well and has the means to do so. That is more than most women get in this life."

"How bleak it seems to be for a woman," said Kit, "To make marital choices based solely on cold financial pragmatism."

"Some very lucky women do not have to choose. Your Miss Adeline for instance. She is free to marry as her heart wills, since her heart has chosen an incredibly wealthy and highly placed man." said the Dowager Duchess with a sly side-glance towards Kit.

"How do you know what her heart has chosen?" asked Kit, not bothering to deny the possibility that he might actually offer for Adeline's hand.

"You think she might not feel for you?" said his mother with some surprise.

Kit shrugged and looked down at his coffee, surprised at the sudden heart-sickness he felt. "As you say, I am powerful and wealthy, a Duke no less. Any woman who married me would shoot up to the pinnacle of society and have as much money and material possessions as she could use in a hundred lifetimes. Even if Ada - Miss Adeline had no affection for me at all, she would still agree to the match. To be a Duchess is too tempting an offer for any woman to turn down."

His mother shrugged. "I suppose you're right. I certainly didn't turn down the opportunity even though I didn't love your father."

"Mother! That is completely unhelpful."

The Dowager Duchess went silent for a moment, considering her response. "Your father was much like you, incredibly handsome, charming, and of course, a Duke. We married because he needed a woman of good-breeding to continue his line, a fact he made very clear during our courtship. But I think, if he had tried to make me fall in love with him, it wouldn't have been difficult."

Kit thought of the man his father had been to his family, cold and dutiful but never cruel, and then of the secret life his father had had with his mistress, a woman he could not marry no matter how much latitude his position gave him in choosing a wife. He'd felt anger though not surprise at learning of this woman his father had maintained for years. But now he wondered, what if the woman had been to his father what Adeline was to him? Perhaps he would have acted no differently to his father in the same situation. But his situation was not the same. The woman he was falling in love with was an acceptable spouse.

"You think she could come to love me?" he asked.

"I think, my darling son, that you can do anything you put your mind to." His mother reached out and patted his hand. "You can have such happiness in your future, you just need to reach out and take it."

"Sorry, sorry I'm late!" Marianne burst in with a swirl of skirts, her children behind her, followed by a frantic looking nursemaid.

His mother's butler squeezed in behind them, "The Marchioness of Reeth, The Earl -" he began to announce.

The Duchess waved him away.

"You're not that late." said mother.

"Actually, you're incredibly late;" interjected Kit, "so late I have to go."

"No Uncle Kit, No!" yelled the children.

Kit scooped up little Isabella and Peter under his arms and swung them around. "Fine, I'll take you to parliament with me. Know what they do with little children there?"

"What?!" they screamed.

"They eat them!"

"No!"

"Oh yes! There's nothing the Lords love more than the taste of human children. They gobble them up like sweets. And I bet you two taste particularly good."

"Gah, no!" the children screamed as he made to take them out the door.

"Kit, stop teasing them. They're already little terrors, they need no help from you," said Marianne.

He put them down.

"It's all right, Uncle Kit, I know we wouldn't really be eaten," said Isabella.

"And why is that?"

"Papa is in paarl- parli- parment and he won't let us be eaten."

"Parliament. And you're right. Your father wouldn't let anything happen to you."

For all Lord Reeth's faults as a husband, he was an excellent father. All the love and attention he withheld from Marianne, he spent lavishly on their children.

"Do you really have to go? I feel like I've hardly seen you since I got to London," said Marianne. With the pout on her face, she was like a younger version of mother. "And what's all this I read in the gossip columns about an Adeline Duefont? Are you getting married, Kit?"

"Now I really have to go. I've already heard it all from mother, I'd rather not stick around to hear it from you too."

"That wasn't a no!" said Marianne.

"I'm not getting married!" said Kit exasperated.

"Marianne, stop teasing your brother and sit down," said the Dowager Duchess.

"Yes Marianne, sit down and mind your own business," said Kit snidely.

Marianne shot him a glare. With great difficulty, and by reminding himself that he was a Duke, Kit resisted sticking out his tongue in response.

"Goodbye little imps," he said, ruffling Peter's curls on his way out, and bending obligingly for a sticky kiss from Isabella.

"Kit darling, don't forget about lunch!" called his mother.

He waved his hand to show he'd heard.

Chapter 10
The Dowager Duchess' Picnic

The weather was perfect for the Dowager Duchess of Aberlay's picnic, as if even the skies did not dare to risk her disapproval. Ladies in pastel pinks, lilacs and yellows dotted around the immaculate lawn of the Aberlay's vast garden, their faces protected from the bright sun by the vast brims of their sun hats. Some had even taken the extra precaution of carrying silk parasols. Ada doubted it would do much good. On a day as glorious as this a little tanning was inevitable.

As expected, the cream of society's ladies were in attendance. By the oak tree stood Lady Jersey, whispering something to Lady Sefton, whose eyes kept darting to a group of young girls that were no doubt the subject of their hushed conversation. Ada recognised the wives of some foreign ambassadors, incongruous due to the bolder colours of their dresses, amongst them a German countess and a Russian princess. And of course, the season's most prominent debutants and their mothers were in attendance, all the young women from the best families, with either good looks, a considerable fortune or both.

Looking at the best women England had to offer, Ada began to feel rather out of place. Hetty with her beautiful features and elegant manners seemed to fit right in, which was no doubt why she and mother had been invited.

"Aren't private picnics during the season just lovely," said Mama, "Why I cannot stand those public affairs in Hyde Park where anyone can get in and there are always people around gawping at you."

She spoke as if they were getting invitations to private picnics thrown at them constantly. "Most people don't have a choice if they wish to picnic," said Ada.

Including us, she added in her head. It was all very well to turn your nose up at public picnics if you had the means to conduct private ones, but the fact was, only the exceedingly well-off had gardens in London large enough to accommodate an event like this.

Her mother ignored her, "Why, there is dear Lady Castlereagh! I had better go greet her." Ada would eat her hat if mama had talked to Lady Castlereagh more than twice in her life. Still the Viscountess, though a little startled, showed no signs of obvious impatience at mama's approach.

"Well, Hetty, it is just you and me then I suppose," said Ada, turning around. There was an empty space where her sister had been moments ago. A quick glance around revealed that Hetty had walked a few paces away and was now in an animated conversation with her future sister-in-law, the Viscountess Beulle. Whatever they were discussing looked serious and Ada was reluctant to be an awkward interloper, particularly if the conversation was centred around Ashbourne and their upcoming nuptials.

Ada sighed. Perhaps there was a group somewhere in this gaggle of girls she could join safely to bide her time until the end of the picnic.

"Miss Adeline Duefont?"

She turned to see an elegant woman dressed in the highest fashion. Sharp blue eyes peered out from beneath a feathered hat that Ada guessed would cost her entire yearly allowance. In fact, the lady was better dressed than anyone here, which was saying something given the quality of the guests. There was something familiar in her face, but Ada was almost certain she'd never met her before.

"I am," she paused, not wanting to offend, "Have we...I'm not sure if we've been introduced."

The woman laughed, "No, no, you needn't strain your brain trying to remember me. I'm terribly forward, I hope you don't mind. I'm Marianne." This was all said in such a lively manner, that Ada couldn't help but be charmed.

"Adeline then, or Ada if you please. But you are very mysterious and have me entirely at a disadvantage. You know who I am, but I have no last name or title for you."

Marianne linked her arm with Ada and laughed again. Ada got the impression this was a woman given to easy laughter. "No mystery, I just find titles so cumbersome for one's friends. And I have a feeling we shall be the closest of friends so there's no use in not starting as we mean to go on."

Ada laughed, "That's all very well, but I still don't know who you really are. So, I stand by my original assessment of your enigmatic nature."

The woman smiled. "The Marchioness of Reeth is how they introduce me in society. See? Most tedious."

This was dropped so casually into the conversation, as if it wasn't worth mentioning, that it took Ada a moment to register the words. She went limp in surprise which only made it easier for the lady to drag her across the lawn. The Marchioness of Reeth. Kit's sister. The resemblance jumped out at her now. The same dark hair and piercing eyes, the same charm and utter confidence. How could she have missed it?

"You're the Duke of Aberlay's sister."

"His older, more attractive, more charming sister. So, if you want embarrassing stories about him, I've got plenty. I, of course, come off extremely well in each retelling."

Ada laughed, "Poor Kit is beleaguered enough already with the society matrons and debutants desperate to be a Duchess. The last thing he needs is embarrassing stories of his youth shared about." Too late she realised she'd referred to the Duke familiarly again. But Marianne made no mention of it. Unlike the Duchess, she seemed to find it perfectly unremarkable that Ada would go around calling her brother by a name only his close friends and family used.

"You don't count yourself amongst their number?"

"Society matrons? Surely, I need to age a couple of decades at least."

"Debutants desperate to be a Duchess."

It was Ada's turn to laugh, "I'm never going to be a Duchess. What's the point of dangling for something unrealistic? The Duke and I are friends. Or at least I consider him a friend." She considered him a lot more than that, and it hurt her to admit that in all likelihood, she was just a casual acquaintance in his grand life.

"Oh, I'm sure Kit considers you a friend at the very least. Besides, none of those girls are going to become a Duchess either and it hasn't stopped them 'dangling' for it as you say."

"Well, I suppose you're right in that he can only make one of them his Duchess so most will lose out. The difference between me and them is that they have a chance."

"Why would you not have a chance?" Marianne asked, her light-hearted tone growing serious.

Ada smiled, "I am neither beautiful nor particularly high-born by the standards of the ton. A Duke can have his pick of anyone."

"Indeed he can. So why not you?"

Ada laughed, the statement was so absurd.

"Marianne darling. There you are," called the Duchess of Aberlay. Ada realised with surprise that the Marchioness had led her straight to the top of the garden. Here the Dowager Duchess sat among the greatest ladies of the ton, their silk skirts spread out over the picnic blanket. A nearby oak cast enough shade over the ensemble for many of the women to remove their bonnets.

"And Adeline dear. Come and sit next to me. Have you met Lady Jersey yet?" said the Dowager Duchess. Ada felt as if she'd slipped and fallen into an alternate reality, where she was apparently friends with a Marchioness and a Duchess treated her like family.

"Yes, the Lady Jersey was kind enough to sign my card for Almack's."

"Oh, it was no kindness," protested the lady, "I could hardly leave the loveliest debutante in London out."

Ada blushed. Were they teasing her? But there was no laughter or even a sly smile on anyone's lips. If anything, The Dowager Duchess looked satisfied. "Quite so," she said, "You've made quite a splash in the social papers dear."

"Well, I'm happy to have been let in," said Adeline.

"Even though the lemonade is flat?" asked the Duchess, an eyebrow raised.

Ada smiled back, "It's part of the charm of Almack's. The best gentlemen, the most accomplished ladies and the flattest lemonade in London."

For a moment she worried she'd given offence. After all, these were two patronesses of the esteemed institution she'd just disparaged. But then the Dowager Duchess burst into laughter and they all followed suit.

"We should put it on the invitations," said Lady Jersey, "The flattest lemonade in London!"

A footman came around with a tray of lemonade. Ada took a glass and a sip.

"Not too flat for you dear?" asked the Duchess.

"Not flat enough!" declared Ada. "I've developed quite a taste for flat lemonade since Almack's."

The Duchess giggled. "I shall speak to my cook and tell her to make adjustments."

"In truth it's delicious," said Ada.

"All Mama's food is. She is excellent at hiring staff. Here, try one of these sweetmeats Ada," said Marianne, passing around a platter.

Ada popped the candy in her mouth and it fizzed pleasantly with the lemonade.

Marianne took off her bonnet and stretched her legs out, her hair the same inky black as Kit's. "La, I just love picnics. Where else can a full-grown lady sit and eat on the floor?"

"There's no reason why you couldn't do it at home if you like it so much," said Ada.

"What? Throw a blanket in the middle of the dining room and insist on having dinner there?" said Marianne, "I'd be institutionalised."

Ada smiled. "Maybe it's the sort of thing you have to build up to gradually. Lots of small eccentric acts until eating dinner on the floor just becomes expected of you."

"How wonderful it must be to be an eccentric," said Marianne, "You can just do as you please and people wave it off and say, 'oh isn't she eccentric,' as opposed to labelling you insane."

"It would not be wonderful to be eccentric," said the Duchess, "Look at Lady Rebecca Fairchild."

"Oh yes, the Earl of Orton's daughter," said Lady Jersey, "Impeccable breeding, pretty enough and yet no respectable man will touch her with a barge pole. She's thirty this year and her parents have quite despaired of her ever marrying."

"Well, if I were a gentleman I think it would be rather fun to marry an eccentric woman," said Marianne.

"Then you could have dinner on the floor every night," said Ada.

Marianne laughed, "Quite so."

The Dowager Duchess shook her head at them but it was done fondly. "I had better do the social rounds. They'll be serving the sandwiches soon and I've hardly talked to my guests," said the Duchess standing up, "Now where did I put my bonnet?"

They all looked around the picnic blanket, but the Duchess's bonnet was nowhere to be found.

"Are you sure you were wearing it when you came out?" asked Marianne.

"Indeed you're right, I wasn't. The footman had a question for me so I came to attend it and then people began to arrive. My bonnet is still in the library."

There were no footmen close by. The Duchess frowned.

"I can fetch it," offered Ada, "I'm still wearing my bonnet anyway."

"Thank you dear, that's very kind," said the Duchess, "The library is down the corridor as you go in, second door to the left."

"You can borrow mine in the meantime Mama," said Marianne, "It'll clash, but that can't be helped."

Ada left her empty glass resting in the grass and walked towards the house. Between the house and garden was a large stone patio with no shade. After hours baking in the sun, it was exceedingly hot. Ada reached the back doors and slipped into the coolness of the house with relief.

The Duchess' home was massive. The corridor three times larger than in the Duefont townhouse. Ada's feet sank into deep carpet with every step. She tried not to feel too much like an interloper. Second door to the left. Ada passed the first and reached the second, turning the cool knob and slipping into the library, shutting the door behind her.

But she wasn't alone. A tall man with a familiar wave of black hair stood at the desk. "Kit," she whispered, startled.

He turned and his eyes locked on hers. Ada's heartbeat accelerated, as it always did near him.

Chapter 11
What Happens in the Library

"What are you doing here?" she asked.

"This is my house."

Ada spluttered, "You have a hundred houses. Probably half a dozen in London alone. What are you doing in this one?"

The Duke raised an eyebrow, "I don't have a *hundred* houses. Maybe eighty or ninety. But does that mean I'm no longer permitted to visit my mother?"

Ada took a moment to process the fact that the Duke had so many houses, he didn't know how many he owned, "If you are indeed visiting your mother, what are you doing holed up in the library? She's in the garden. I can take you to her if you wish."

"Absolutely not. Don't think you'll trick me so easily. I'm not letting you finish off my mother's nearly successful scheme. I know exactly who else is in that garden. Just about every young, marriageable woman in London."

Ada's eyes widened, "The Duchess invited us here for a comfortable, all-female picnic."

"Indeed," said Kit darkly, "Framing the invite that way means I'll be the only man here. It's already carnage in a ballroom when both sexes are equally represented. Can you imagine the slaughter if I'm the only male representative amongst all those eager women?"

It was true. Kit was already hounded wherever he went by any unmarried woman between sixteen and thirty-five, not to mention their mothers, "Why on earth did you agree to come?" Ada asked aghast.

"You think I agreed to this?" asked the Duke incredulously, "Come over for a quiet lunch with your dear mama, is what she told me. No mention of any other guest, let alone the fifty odd women I find camped out on the lawn. 'Dear mama' indeed! What woman with a shred of maternal instinct could do this to her own son?"

Ada couldn't help a giggle at his dramatics, she stifled it quickly but not before the Duke shot her a glare. "It's not funny," he said.

"No of course not," said Ada with a twitch of her lips, "The mighty and all-powerful Duke of Aberlay, decorated war hero and leader of the ton, hiding in the library.

The Duke smiled then and Ada couldn't help notice how it brightened his entire face. "I've always thought that sending a few of the ton's matrons to the front lines would've sent Napoleon packing quicker than any assault our troops could muster. They are terrifying."

They stood smiling at each other for just long enough for Ada to feel self-conscious. "Well, I'd better get back to those terrifying matrons. I only came to fetch the Dowager Duchess's hat," she said, locating the wide, feathered bonnet on a side table.

"Or you could stay?" said Kit.

Ada had already turned to leave, but she looked back at him in surprise.

"When the butler told me what was going on, I asked for a light selection of food to be sent to the library. I'd already told my housekeeper not to prepare lunch," said the Duke. He suddenly seemed very awkward, but he cleared his throat and continued, "As you can see, he sent rather a lot. Perhaps you would join me? That is, if you want to?"

The Duke gestured towards the table and on it was a large plate of triangular sandwiches along with a tea set and some pastries that looked so delicious Ada's mouth began to water.

"Maybe just for a while," said Ada. It was probably not exactly appropriate, but she was suddenly hungry and the thought of spending time in a quiet library with Kit was hugely appealing.

He sat down behind the desk, and she took the armchair opposite. The table was just small enough that their knees pressed together underneath. Sunlight flooded through the room's large windows, falling on the table and giving the room the glow of a summer's day. Ada reached for a sandwich.

"So why is your mother so eager to get you married off anyway? Most men wait until their thirties, and you don't look that old to me," she said, taking a large bite. The sharp taste of radishes, combined with cucumbers and smoked salmon hit her taste buds. The Dowager Duchess really did have an excellent cook.

"You're right. I'll only be six and twenty this year. Unfortunately for me, the Dukes of Aberlay have not been particularly prolific," said Kit, taking a bite of his own sandwich, "and to exacerbate the problem, it's a relatively new Dukedom, I'm only the fourth holder of this title. Which means there aren't a lot of distant relatives either who can fill in if necessary. I think there are only two male cousins in line to inherit. And neither have male children yet."

"Hence the need for you to wed as soon as possible and get started on being more prolific than your ancestors."

"Exactly," said the Duke with a wry grin, "I wonder that my father and mother didn't do a better job of populating the Aberlay succession tree," A bitterness crept into his voice, "Even though they had no particular affection for each other, it seldom got in the way of them doing their duty," He paused and shook his head slightly, "Sorry, I shouldn't mention it. They were perfectly proper parents to me and my sister so I shouldn't make any complaints."

"It's all right. I understand. There isn't much love lost between my parents either," said Ada, giving him a truth of her own to balance the scales, "My mother is the daughter of a Baron. She expected to marry into the same social rank as her father. But a lack of offers meant she had to accept the hand of a mere country baronet. She is dissatisfied with her lot and makes no effort to disguise it, and her dissatisfaction makes Papa dissatisfied in turn. I often think he would have been happier married to a woman of the lower gentry."

"He made his choice based on money rather than affection."

"It seems most couples in the ton do," said Ada.

"And you?" asked Kit, "is that how you would make your choice also?"

"In truth, I would like a grand love match. I think most women would. In that regard at least, I envy Hetty and Ashbourne. But I think I could settle for affection. As for money, I do not have high expectations. Enough to live on I suppose."

"And what is enough to live on for Miss Adeline Duefont? A four-horse phaeton, a set of diamond jewels for each day of the week, new brocade gowns for every occasion?" he teased.

Adeline laughed, "Don't forget a constant supply of new silk slippers and feathered hats."

"Of course. How remiss of me," said Kit with a smile. He shifted slightly and his calf rubbed along the inside of Ada's leg with the motion. She suppressed a shiver.

"In all seriousness, I would be happy enough to live the life of the gentry. No seasons in London, or multiple homes, or anything like that. Just enough for a single, well-maintained house. I do not have high expectations for myself." She swallowed and looked down. Next to Kit, with his handsome features and the status he wore like a mantle, she suddenly felt plain and inconsequential. What was she doing conversing like this with a Duke? He was so far above her.

Kit reached out and took her hand. Ada startled at the contact, lifting her gaze to where her small hand was encased in his. She wasn't wearing gloves. This wasn't an evening ball after all. So she felt acutely the roughness of his thumb as it brushed over her palm, the heat radiating from his tanned fingers as they entangled with hers. Ada's breathing sped up and little bolts of lightning shot through her from where they touched.

"Why do you do that? Act as if you are less?"

Ada tried to put on a smile but it felt brittle. "My mother always had it fixed that Hetty was the pretty one and I was plain. Hetty has light hair and takes after Mama's sisters. Whereas my colouring is darker and more unattractive."

"Darker, yes, but not unattractive. Exotic, alluring, beautiful, those words describe you better."

Ada flushed. "You are flattering me."

"No. I state only the truth. Your sister is pretty enough, but nothing compared to you Ada. When you enter a room you're all I can look at. You're beautiful."

To hear these words coming from Kit. Ada didn't think her heart could take it. She told herself firmly that he was only being kind, gentlemanly. After all, he could hardly agree that a lady was plain and unattractive even if she was. She shook her head.

"Ada, what can I say to make you understand." His grip tightened around her hand, "There are many who agree with me. Whatever your mother told you she is wrong. I would not change a single thing about your appearance. By far you are the most beautiful woman -"

The library doors burst open. Ada turned to see the Dowager Duchess standing in the doorway.

The Duke dropped her hand and stood up abruptly, "Mama I was just -"

"Alone in a room with a young, unmarried lady and nary a chaperone in sight. Based on when I last spoke to Miss Adeline, this private tête-à-tête has been going on for close to an hour."

Ada stood up too, her face turning bright red. How awful and humiliating. She opened her mouth to form some sort of reply, probably starting with an embarrassing apology, when the Duke stepped in front of her. Although it probably wasn't done for that reason, Ada felt instantly protected.

"This is entirely my doing. I prevailed upon Miss Adeline's company and it is because of her good nature and agreeableness that we are in this situation. The lady is innocent of any wrong. Mama, you will tell no one of this."

Ada held her breath. With a single word, the Dowager Duchess could ruin Ada's life forever. She wouldn't even have to say anything about Ada's unchaperoned encounter with her son. All the Dowager Duchess had to do was cut Ada and her family. No explanation required. The rest of the ton would quickly follow suit, such was the power she held in society. She would deserve it too. Shame and sadness welled up in Ada. The Dowager Duchess had been kind to her, and Ada had liked her very much in return. Now that was all at an end.

"Both of you will never breathe a word of what transpired here to anyone, and neither shall I," said the Duke's mother firmly, "No one knows you are here, Kit, apart from the staff. You will leave directly before any of the guests see you. As for Adeline," said the Dowager Duchess, coming around her son to face Ada directly, "We will return together and tell them an elaborate story of how I found you searching the entire house for my bonnet which wasn't in any of the places I told you it would be."

Ada could hardly believe it. The Dowager Duchess, strict patroness of Almack's who wrote the book on the rules of society, was helping them get away with a huge breach of propriety.

"Did anyone see you on your way to the library? Any of the servants?" asked the Dowager Duchess as she led Ada away.

"No. No one."

"Then we are safe. As far as I am concerned it never happened."

"Thank you. I should have stopped it," said Ada.

"You know, if anyone else had found you, you would be engaged by now," said the Duchess.

Ada went pale. The Duchess was right. Effectively, she had been compromised. Even if nothing had happened. Unlike last time. She brushed that memory away quickly. What would the Duchess think of her now? It looked as if she'd tried to trap Kit into marriage. And the last thing Her

Grace could want was Ada for a daughter-in-law. "I'm sorry. I would never want to force his hand."

The Duchess laughed. "Force his hand? My dear, I don't think any force is required. You needn't apply force to an object already in motion."

"I don't understand," said Ada.

The older woman turned to look at her, taking in Ada's puzzled expression. "You really have no concept of your own charms, do you? How delightful."

Ada might have questioned this curious statement, but they had reached the garden and one of her guests drew the Duchess away.

Chapter 12
The Beulle Ball

Some days had passed since Hetty and Ashbourne's wedding and by now the happy couple would be somewhere in Scotland on their Honeymoon. Ada felt the loss of her sister keenly. She was still getting used to waking up in an empty room, with none of Hetty's morning prattling to keep her company. It was hard to remain ill-tempered in the face of her sister's happiness, and even Mama had begrudgingly managed a cheerful countenance to see her oldest daughter off.

But now with the wedding over, all of Mama's considerable attention focused on Ada. New fittings, appearances at the Opera in Aunt Caroline's box, mandatory morning walks in Hyde Park, trips to Vauxhall pleasure gardens, and of course, attending every ball they held an invitation to.

Ada estimated she got through at least three changes of clothes a day, and it was exhausting and expensive. Tonight would be no exception. It was the Viscount and Viscountess Beulle's annual spring ball, and with Hetty's marriage to Ashbourne, of course the Duefonts were invited. They were family now, no matter the circumstances that led there.

"The blue silk, no, the pink," said Mama.

It took some effort not to sigh.

"And flowers. Not the roses."

Ada allowed Mama to dress her how she wanted. Or rather, order the maids to dress her. She knew from experience her opinions were neither required nor wanted. Instead she thought about Kit, as she often did when her mind wandered. She'd glimpsed him accompanying his sister about town, and they'd danced together at the Dermot ball. Although the nature of the dance had left little opportunity for conversation, she smiled remembering the way his arms had encircled her, the brush of his thumb against her waist, the small smile on his face that always made Ada's pulse pick up.

"You are thinking of Mr Mellford," said Mama, "I can tell by that smile on your face.

Ada startled. She probably should be thinking of Mellford. The man had been incredibly attentive to her in the last week and unlike the Duke, there was a serious chance he would propose marriage.

"Six thousand a year is very comfortable," continued Mama, "He can afford to give you seasons in London, a good allowance for your pin money, and if his uncle dies without children, Mellford might be a Baron one day!"

"Mama I hardly think we should be so enthusiastic about the death of Mellford's uncle."

Lady Deufont sniffed. "Well, I was only saying."

Her mother wasn't wrong. Mellford was a good match for Ada. Better than she'd thought she could get at the start of the season. He wasn't bad to look at, although he certainly wasn't going to turn heads like Kit. Mellford also wasn't too old, had a full head of hair and was able to hold a decent conversation. He was everything Ada could hope for in a husband. She should accept him if he offered and forget all about the Duke.

"I am sure he will be at tonight's ball," said Mama. "The Duke?"

Mama gave her an odd look and Ada wished she could stuff the words back into her mouth. "No. Mr Mellford of course. Why would I be talking about the Duke of Aberlay?"

"I was thinking of Hetty I suppose. And the circumstances of her marriage," said Ada.

"Hmpf. Well, I suppose he will be there. It seems the Duke is a great friend of Viscount Beulle if he sees fit to interfere in the marriage prospects of the man's brother."

"You cannot still be upset about that Mama. Hetty and Ashbourne are happy and a Viscount's brother is a good choice. Not even daughters of Lords always get to marry peers. There just aren't enough to go around."

Mama pursed her lips and Ada for a second time found herself wishing to take back her words. She hadn't meant it as a comment on Mama's own marriage, but of course that is precisely how it had been perceived.

Kit supposed he and Viscount Beulle were friends now. The man certainly thought so from the way he'd thumped Kit across the shoulder at White's and all but demanded he make an appearance at his ball. Not that Kit would have skipped it anyway. With Henrietta Duefont married into the family, Ada was sure to be there, and lately he'd found himself unable to stay away from any place she was likely to be. This ballroom was no exception.

He tugged on his waistcoat, then examined his cuffs. His tailor had done a good job. He always did.

His sister, who he was accompanying, laughed. "She will be here soon enough. No need to fret."

"I do not fret," said Kit.

"No, of course not. You must be having terrible trouble with your clothes then. You've checked your cuffs three times since we arrived, and adjusted your waistcoat twice as much," said Marianne.

Manderville materialised beside them.

"Ah, Lord Manderville," greeted Marianne, "I don't suppose you could recommend a tailor? Kit is having the most awful results with his."

"Yes, indeed I can. You'll observe how I haven't needed to adjust my waistcoat a single time unlike poor Kit here," said Manderville, neatly picking up where Marianne left off, "He's an excellent chap, just off Bond street -"

"My tailor is fine," said Kit, "Honestly. Did the two of you get together in secret to plan this?"

"If I was meeting with Marianne in secret, talking about you would be the last thing on my mind," said Manderville, his voice dropping suggestively.

He would've felt vaguely sick at that statement, except at that precise moment, Adeline walked into the ballroom. She was in pink silk today with cherry blossoms in her hair, and more pinned to the shoulder of her dress. Beautiful. Kit was seized with a desire to feel those flowers against his lips and then trail down across the creamy expanse of her exposed neck, and down to her chest, where just the top swell of her breasts were visible. He wanted to hold her in his arms and run his hands all over her body. He wanted her to want him with the same desperate longing he felt when he looked at her.

But it wasn't lust alone. And affection was insufficient to describe it. Even if he could never touch her body, he would be content only to talk with her, to find happiness in her mere presence. He lived for the rare moments when he shocked a laugh out of her, or when she sent him a teasing smile that inevitably shot straight to his heart. Despite his best attempts, with each passing day his affection, his desire for her only grew.

Somewhere deep in the recesses of Kit's heart, affection had turned to love. Impossible to deny. It thundered through his body whenever he looked at her, filling his veins, his capillaries, every fibre of his being. Kit welcomed the flood of emotion. Hadn't he known from the first moment he saw her that she had the potential to make him feel like this? He'd been a fool to think this would pass.

Marriage. It was the logical next step. But Ada had said she wanted to fall in love. Kit had heard those words and desperately wanted her to love him. Repeating a marriage like his parents, dutiful and cold, was undesirable in the extreme. He didn't think he could do it, and if he could, it would hurt him immensely, because no matter how cold Ada came to be towards him, Kit knew he would love her forever.

"Watch out," said Manderville, "Looks like you have a rival for the fair lady's hand."

A stout man with blond curls and a bright beam on his face bowed before Ada. She blushed, bestowing the man with a grin of her own and something in Kit shattered. Had Ada ever smiled at him like that? Never so widely or openly, her eyes sparkling and her face flushed with pleasure.

"Who is he?" Kit asked.

"Mr Mellford I think," said Marianne.

"Tell me what you know about him?"

"Well let's see," said his sister, "He's the grandson of a Baron. Inherited six thousand a year from his father. And if he's very lucky, his uncle might die without children, leaving him a Barony. All in all, very respectable."

"He might not inherit the Barony then," said Kit.

Marianne shrugged, "He still has six thousand a year."

And that was the rub of it. An impoverished gentleman might be turned down for practical reasons. But Adeline had no reason to reject this Mr Mellford. Not if she liked him better. Which it looked like she did. Kit startled at the shock of pain when she put her hand on Mr Mellford's arm. The gentleman looked delighted, and well he should. What red-blooded man wouldn't be pleased to have Adeline smiling and flirting with him?

"Relax old boy. It doesn't matter if she prefers him now," said Manderville.

Realising his fists had clenched involuntarily, Kit forced his body into a more relaxed pose. But that did nothing to quiet his turmoil. He turned on Manderville. "Because I am a Duke you mean. My fortune and title will be too tempting to turn down. Even if she loves another."

Manderville raised an eyebrow at his tone. "I just meant you can charm her. Make her prefer you instead. Smile at her occasionally. Don't be such a bore. Tell her a joke. That sort of thing."

"A difficult task for my brother perhaps," said Marianne dryly.

Kit shot her a quelling look and then his shoulders slumped. "You are right. I am too serious. Without my title and wealth there isn't much for a woman to like."

Manderville slapped him hard across the shoulders, shocking Kit into straightening up. "See this is exactly what I said not to do. You're being a bore. No woman wants to hear how hard life is as a wealthy, powerful Duke. At least no sensible one. Talk about something light-hearted. Use your face."

"My face?"

"It's not completely horrible looking?" said Manderville, glancing at Marianne for confirmation.

"Yes. I think we can agree that you have a passable face. Children don't run away screaming or anything like that," said his sister supportively. She paused for a moment as if thinking. "At least my children don't. But now I think of it, that could just be from familiarity."

"I've read about that," said Manderville, "Desensitisation to the morbid."

They both turned to look at him as if to actually examine his face.

"Thank you," said Kit, "You're both extremely helpful. Just what one needs in a crisis of self-confidence."

"Anytime," said Manderville brightly. He turned to Marianne, "Would you care to dance?"

They left him there. And without either Marianne or Manderville engaging him in conversation, Kit was soon accosted by some lady with three daughters. He extracted himself with only a little difficulty and quickly fled through the wide doors that led into the Beulle's garden. The only woman he cared to dance with was already occupied. He spared Ada one last glance as she twirled in Mellford's arms.

The dimly-lit patio held more than a few couples seeking privacy away from the ballroom. Kit wanted no part of it. He descended the steps into the garden proper, his boots crunching across the lawn until the lights from the party faded and only the half-moon's glow remained. He looked up at it and wondered if it too felt incomplete.

Kit scoffed at himself. Pathetic. His father had been right all those years ago. Seeking love in marriage was a fool's errand. At least for a Duke. If Ada had the choice of him or Mr Mellford, she might choose him, but only for his title and wealth. He'd vaguely noted Mellford before. He was often amongst Ada's dance partners and part of the general crowd of gentlemen that gathered around her. But he'd been so preoccupied with his own feelings, he'd never taken the time to observe them together properly. And now he had, there was no denying it, thought Kit with a pang. The way she smiled at Mellford, the way she opened up herself to him, touched him so casually. Mellford was the one who held Ada's affections.

Kit couldn't ask Ada to marry him now. It was impossible. Her socially conscious parents might force her to choose him against her own preferences. And even if she picked him of her own volition, it wouldn't be for the right reasons, for the reason Kit wanted it to be. He doubted she would though. Ada had told him she didn't want London seasons or extravagant gowns, a man of good character and a modest home in the country would be enough to ensure her happiness. From another woman he would have thought it a bluff, but Ada had spoken sincerely. God, he loved her. And he would have to live with her marrying someone else. That was the decent thing. The right thing.

"Kit?"

Her voice. He would know it anywhere. Turning, he saw her staring at him. Silhouette only just visible in the dark, her eyes unusually bright. He looked at her, desire and anger mingling within him and decency was the last thing on his mind.

"Are you going to marry him?" he spat out. A wildly inappropriate question he had no right to ask.

"Mellford?"

"Who else?"

"I suppose so. Yes. If he asks me." It was as he'd expected. But hearing it directly from her was a chain-shot fired at his heart.

"What are you doing here then? Dear Mellford not entertaining enough? Perhaps you are here for a different kind of entertainment?" Kit could hear the vitriol in his tone but was unable to stop it.

"What do you mean?" she asked, "What else would I be here for?"

"What else indeed," said Kit, moving closer to her than any dance would allow, "We both know how much you enjoy my kisses. You made it clear the night Ashbourne ruined your sister that you wouldn't be opposed to being ruined yourself."

She audibly gasped, face flushing red. And this was all wrong. Where Mellford had made her colour in pleasure, he was hurting her. But something cruel within him wanted her to feel at least a fraction of the pain she'd caused him, and that part revelled in the flash of hurt across her features.

"We were playing a part."

"Ah yes, my seductive mistress, and how good you were at it too," he said, running the back of his hand slowly across her cheek, under her jaw and resting it finally against the base of her neck. A proprietary touch. "So responsive. So willing to please me. A man might believe you wished to be my mistress for real."

"I-I don't. I wouldn't," she gasped out.

And of course she wouldn't. Adeline was a respectable woman of good character. The granddaughter of a Baron with twenty thousand pounds to her name. Kit should never be treating her like this. No gentleman would. He should step away. Instead he said, "Yes you would. It wasn't acting. I bet you'd respond exactly the same now."

He tugged her forward by the nape of her neck and slanted his mouth over hers. Ada made a small sound, as if in protest, but Kit didn't let it develop into outright rejection. He deepened the kiss almost immediately, pressing into her mouth. A brief moment of resistance and then she was giving in. Clutching at him, her hands curled around his coat jacket, drawing him closer.

Kit moulded her against his body, pressing his hardness into her curves. He wanted her to remember the imprint of him. To know that when she married Mellford, Kit had been the first to kiss her, the first one to stoke the flames of desire within her. He kissed her bottom lip, slow and agonising and then her upper lip, before coaxing open her mouth, so he could lick inside, hot, wet and desperate. Ada trembled against him, and then shocked Kit by sucking on his tongue. The blood rushed to his groin so fast it left him light-headed.

He groaned. More aroused than he'd ever been in his life, from a simple kiss. His hands, greedy now, traced the length of her body, until at last his fingertips reached the swell of her breasts, just visible over the neckline of her dress. 'Go no further' the rational part of his mind urged. But Kit was beyond reason. His senses filled only with Ada, her touch, her feminine scent, her intoxicating taste.

His questing fingers slipped under, cupping firmly the rounded flesh as if he had every right. A thief taking what wasn't his. She let out a small gasp and Kit gentled the kiss, seeking to soothe as well as arouse. The pad of his thumb brushed over her nipple and this time they both gasped. He was gripped with the urge to tear her bodice away and take that sensitive peak in his mouth, worry it with his tongue and then continue further down, slaking his claim on her body like an animal.

"Kit," she breathed. It was barely a word but it caused him to pull away enough to look at her. Their spit-slick lips parted and she looked at him wide-eyed, pupils dilated with arousal. It was this look of innocence that shocked him away from the hot edge of passion. Because she was an innocent. That much was evident, and here Kit was, groping at her like a back-alley whore. Shame and horror replaced desire.

Chapter 13
Afterwards

Ada's heart beat a fierce rhythm in her chest. She should have stopped him ten minutes ago, or even better, not come outside looking for him at all. She could admit to herself that needing fresh air was an excuse. Seeing the Duke leave the ballroom, Ada was gripped with the urge to follow. Perhaps there were gently-bred ladies who could resist such desires. But Ada would challenge them with the image of the Duke standing in the moonlight, straight and aloof as always, his handsome features thrown into sharp relief.

She made no move to stop him when he leaned in for a kiss. Could a marble statue do any better? His firm lips slid over hers and it was as earth-shattering as last time, sending every nerve-ending in her lips ablaze. He tugged her against him and Ada went as easily as a marionette on string.

It was less gentle than last time, need making them rough. Ada exhaled on a gasp and Kit was right there to catch it with his lips. His mouth moving sinfully against hers, claiming it for his own. Ada trembled, desire sending goosebumps all across her body, making the core of her clench up all tight and then melt. His hands which she was so aware of moved, hot fingers sliding under the thin covering of her dress, and suddenly he was cupping the naked weight of her breast in his palm, rubbing the rough pad of his thumb across her over-sensitised nipple.

This would have been the time to stop him. He was touching her somewhere no lady of quality should allow, but instead she arched into it, relishing the sensation of his large, warm hand against her flesh.

It was scandalous. It was wrong. It was the most incredible Ada had ever felt.

"Kit," whispered Ada, unsure if she was pleading with him to stop or keep going. She felt his hot breath against her lips, and it took a moment to register he was no longer kissing her.

"Ada," his voice was deeper than she'd ever heard it and trembled almost as if he were in pain. He moved back slightly, disengaging their mouths and Ada opened her eyes to look at him. He was looking back at her slightly wide-eyed, shocked at her behaviour. Ada flushed, this time in embarrassment rather than passion. He must think her a lightskirt now. She had acted just like the wanton he claimed she was. Ada knew no lady should ever allow a man such liberties, and God, his hand was still cupping her breast as if he had every right to do so. She looked down, mortified, and the Duke seemed to realise at the same time, for he quickly withdrew his hand, and cleared his throat.

"Allow me to extend my deepest apologies. My behaviour is no reflection on your character, Miss Adeline. This was a terrible mistake." It was said so stiffly with none of his previous warmth. He was no longer Kit, but the icy and aloof Duke of Aberlay. A creature Ada couldn't touch or even presume to know.

He bowed stiffly and left her. Ada felt the inexplicable urge to burst into tears. Something she hadn't done in years. Humiliation and despair gave way to anger. Even her mother's casually cruel remarks couldn't induce Ada to cry, what right had this man to such an emotional reaction from her. Yes, she had acted inappropriately with a man who was never going to marry her, but from all she had seen of the Duke, he wasn't the sort of man to go about ruining a debutante's reputation. No one but the two of them would know of this.

Ada was free to find a kind gentleman who would marry her. Probably Mellford, who was a good prospect and close enough to Ada's social station that a proposal would be reasonable to expect. She had to be practical. The plain-faced daughter of a Baronet could not aspire to a brilliant match, let alone the match of the decade. And yes, now that the Duke thought her a light-skirt, a woman of easy virtue, he was unlikely to have anything further to do with Ada. She ignored the pang in her chest. It was for the best. The Duke of Aberlay was a distraction she couldn't afford.

"Mr Mellford had two dances with you. And I'm sure he would've asked a third time if it wasn't tantamount to a proposal. Which I am sure is coming soon too," said Mama, delighted at her daughter's evening.

Ada had slipped back into the bright lights of the ballroom, sure that the evidence of her wantonness was clearly visible for all to see. But no one had remarked on her appearance in any way. Not even Mama who was always so quick with opinions on Ada's appearance.

"Lord Beulle is coming this way," said Mama, "I suppose they are our relations now and we must endure them."

As if being related to a Viscount was a hardship. Mama was still sour about Hetty's marriage and wasn't inclined to look favourably on the men who brought it about. Luckily for Ashbourne's brother, his status as a Viscount meant Mama would never dare snipe at him. Papa was not so lucky. Since the wedding, dinners at the Duefont townhouse had grown particularly unpleasant, with Mama flinging subtle and not-so-subtle barbs across the table. Really she should be most upset at the Duke. After all, it was the Duke who'd brought about the whole arrangement, and exerted enough social pressure on Papa that he could not refuse. But to insult the Duke would be tantamount to insulting God. Exile from the ton and from heaven would be the fruits of both. And at least with God, one could hope for forgiveness.

"Lady Duefont. Miss Duefont," greeted Lord Buelle.

"How lovely your ball is Lord Beulle. I must commend you on your preparations," said Mama, all politeness now.

"The credit is due to Lady Buelle. I provide the funds and then stay well out of it all."

"Well, clearly that strategy has worked very well. If I see Lady Buelle I'll be sure to give her my compliments," said Ada.

The conversation drifted towards Ashbourne and Hetty. Talk of their travel plans and if the newly-wed couple would return to London before the end of the season. Neither of them had received letters from either yet, so it was all speculation at this point.

"Would you care to dance, Miss Duefont?" asked Viscount Buelle.

"Of course," replied Ada.

Having no brothers, this was the closest Ada would ever come to dancing with a male relative. It was strangely comforting. There was no pressure to make conversation or to be charming. After all, they were related now through marriage.

"I understand I am soon to offer congratulations," said Lord Buelle as the opening steps of the dance began.

"What do you mean?" asked Ada.

"Well, I don't mean to overstep. But based on his actions, it is quite obvious to me that you'll be receiving a proposal soon."

Was Mellford really so close to offering? They had danced maybe half a dozen times and had a few conversations, but perhaps that was enough for a gentleman to decide. Mama and Lord Beulle both seemed to think so.

"I had not realised. It didn't seem so obvious to me," said Ada.

"My dear, what other reason could a man have to intervene so? I know Aberlay is fabulously rich, but to drop ten thousand pounds on my brother. And it would have been more. The Duke was going to pay the full twenty thousand. I insisted on giving at least half. Although even that sum stretched my pocketbook."

Lord Buelle was talking about Kit not Mellford thought Ada with astonishment, and yet that was still not the most astonishing part of his statement.

"The Duke was going to give Ashbourne and Hetty twenty thousand pounds?"

"If you don't stop gawping, people will think I've said something very salacious. I thought you knew. Didn't he say?"

With difficulty Ada smoothed her expression into something more neutral. "No. He didn't mention it."

"Very odd. You'd think the man would at least seek credit for such a magnanimous gesture. It hardly helps his case if you remain ignorant of it all. How will you be impressed by his largess and generosity of spirit?"

"How indeed. Perhaps that's not why he did it."

"Nonsense dear. What other reason could he possibly have?"

"I think he felt sorry for Hetty and Ashbourne," said Ada, "He told me as much. Their plight is a sympathetic one. Perhaps he acted out of pity."

"You might be the first person ever to accuse the Duke of sentimentality. The man is known for his coldness. Many women have tried to engage his emotions and failed miserably. Most men with only a fraction of his wealth and status would have associated with a string of mistresses by now. But not a whisper of any of it on Aberlay."

He mistook Ada's silence for shock.

"Forgive me," he said, "Sarah, Lady Buelle, is forever telling me I am too forward. I should not have mentioned, that is, it is a delicate matter and you are an unmarried young lady."

"No please, I have taken no offence. We are family after all and I appreciated you being forthright. It is a lot to think on."

"I'll say. It's not every day a girl becomes a Duchess. And the Duke of Aberlay at that! You couldn't do better if you married the prince. Of the two, Aberlay has the larger fortune."

The level of wealth was unimaginable. A man richer than royalty. Kit seemed further out of reach than ever. She should stick to Mellford and abandon any foolish notions of the Duke. "I think you mistake kindness for admiration, Lord Buelle. As you said, ten or even twenty thousand might be a whole fortune for us, but it is a small sum to him."

"There are certainly better ways of giving to charity Miss Duefont, if that was his intention."

"I do not deny that the personal connection likely formed a large part of his motivation but you make the leap from sympathy to affection too readily, Lord Buelle. He is the Duke of Aberlay after all. When he chooses a bride it will be the daughter of some great Lord or an heiress. Mere mortals do not aspire to the heights of angels."

"Perhaps you are more angel than mortal then," said Lord Buelle, "You have many admirers amongst the ton who would say so. But the men mostly stay away out of respect for Aberlay."

"Well I wish they would not. And that they would stop assuming things. Aberlay is a friend. But he will never marry me. I am glad Mr Mellford at least has not been scared away."

"That man is too infatuated to be sensible."

Ada had a sharp retort ready. Mellford seemed eminently sensible to her and was a far more likely husband than a Duke, but the dance had come to an end so Lord Buelle had the last word. It wouldn't do to be heard arguing with her brother-in-law anyway, especially not about the Duke of Aberlay.

Ada had not realised speculation about their relationship was causing marriage-minded men to actively avoid her for fear of offending the powerful Duke. And were they wrong? Ada blushed as a traitorous part of her mind brought to the forefront the kiss they had shared moments ago. Two kisses in the space of weeks, and the library incident which had just been conversation, but might as well have been more for how intimate it felt. Hadn't Ada pressed her knee up against the Duke's leg, and held his hand with her ungloved one? Sat far closer to him than propriety allowed, close enough to smell his rich masculine scent and see the way his eyes crinkled when he smiled. No wonder the Duke called her a wanton, and now other members of the ton were picking up on it too. How long before Ada ruined her reputation all together?

"Adeline dear you look flushed," said Mama, as Lord Buelle deposited her back, "Too much dancing perhaps. A lemonade will cool you down."

Ada murmured her assent absentmindedly and allowed Mama to lead her forward. She could not be in the Duke's presence any more. Her feelings made it difficult to behave properly around him. One heady look and Ada smouldered, the briefest touch of his sent all reason and sense fleeing. Complete avoidance would be the best course. She should probably tell him at least. Not the part about how she desired him with an engulfing passion. That Ada would take to her grave. But the part where he was scaring away other gentlemen and perhaps Kit could stop asking her to dance so much, and stop talking to her so much, and stop running his hands over her body in a way that made her want to climb all over him. Oh dear, she needed to end that thought right there.

"Here. Drink this," said Mama, thrusting a glass into Ada's hand. "You look quite red. Are you sure you aren't coming down with something?"

"Quite sure, Mama. It's the heat I think." She took a long gulp of lemonade, scanning the ballroom over the rim of her glass. But the Duke of Aberlay, normally so prominent in any room, was missing. He wasn't amongst the dancing couples, nor was he standing on the sides. Ada spotted Marianne, who Kit had accompanied, but of the woman's brother there was no sign. Well, he was a Duke and there were probably a great many demands on his time. Perhaps he'd left early to attend to some matter. Never mind, Ada would tell him another time.

But another time never arrived. After the Buelle ball, Ada looked for the Duke in Hyde Park on her morning walks, but he never appeared. She thought to see him at Almack's, but while the Duchess of Aberlay was there as always, her son was conspicuously absent. At Lady Seely's ball, at Lord Ronceval's ball, at Count Monticello's soirée, Ada had searched in vain for his familiar face, and found it absent. The last occasion being particularly surprising, Count Monticello being a key figure in his country's fight against Napoleon, an issue Ada knew Kit cared deeply about.

From the newspapers, which she had begun reading obsessively, she knew Kit was still in town. He sat in the House of Lords daily, never missing a session and Ada read his speeches with an embarrassing devotion, hearing in her head the way he would pronounce each word with his deep voice. He still appeared in the gossip rags too, an appearance at White's, a bet placed on a horse race, in fact he appeared in almost every social event in which Ada, for reasons of her gender would be excluded. And there were probably other events, unmentioned in these papers, where she would be excluded because of her status. Parties like the masked one she'd attended with Hetty and Ashbourne, where the Duke would dance with a very different kind of lady. Women who would take him to bed with a seductive smile. She swallowed hard and told herself it didn't matter. Anyway, she had Mellford to pay attention to.

Unlike the Duke of Aberlay, of Mr Mellford there was no lack. He seemed to be everywhere Ada was. Always reserving at least one dance at the balls, often the first one. Regularly accompanying her walking and tonight he would be joining Ada's family at the theatre. Mama was beside herself with glee. Her favourite topic of conversation was when Mr Mellford would propose, for it could not be long now. Ada tried to share some of this excitement. Wasn't this everything she set out to achieve at the start of her season? A man of good character and good breeding. And Mellford had money too. Six thousand a year was nothing to sneer at. But whenever she thought of marriage and a husband, her mind strayed and instead of Mellford, she saw Kit standing in his place.

"Adeline hurry! Lord Trefasser and Caroline will be there already," said Mama.
Grabbing her shawl, Ada followed Papa and Mama into the carriage.

Thanks to Aunt Caroline, or rather her husband, Adeline would get to sit in one of the boxes. Aunt Caroline attended the theatre often, but invited her sister a lot less often. It was understandable. While Ada was sure Aunt Caroline loved them, she had a daughter of her own to marry off. Cousin Lavinia, bless her, was not aesthetically gifted and more bluestocking than belle of the ball. And having the same colouring as Hetty, when the two stood together, men paid little attention to Lavinia unless they were after her dowry. Ada didn't think it a coincidence that only after Hetty's wedding did Aunt Caroline extend an offer to share her box.

Mellford was already inside, making polite conversation with Lavinia. His face lit up when Ada walked in and she tried to imitate his enthusiasm.

"You are a vision for sore-eyes," said Mellford, bowing over her hand.

"You look well also Mr Mellford," said Ada, noting his smart breeches and new jacket, probably purchased for the occasion.

"Your arrival is timely. I thought they would start without you," Mellford paused colouring, "That is to say, you are not late. It is no criticism of your tardiness. Uh, lack of tardiness. Your promptness."

Ada laughed, "It's quite all right. I know you intend no offence. We are perpetually late or on the verge of being late. My family, we always start with the best intentions, but somehow the time runs away from us. I can't fault you for stating what is the truth."

"And I can assert to it most definitely being the truth," said Lavinia, "Having known them all my life."

"Yes, poor Lavinia has lost hours waiting for me and Hetty," said Ada, "Do you remember the agricultural fair in Goostrey?"

"How could I forget! I ended up holding that pig for an hour waiting for you," said Lavinia.

"Well, I would gladly wait hours for you Miss Duefont," said Mellford.

"But would you wait hours holding a pig?" asked Lavinia.

Ada shot her a look. Lavinia's expression was one of practised innocence, but she was most definitely poking fun at Mr Mellford.

"Perhaps we should take our seats?" Ada said, neatly saving Mellford from a reply.

Lord and Lady Trefasser's private theatre box was lushly decorated. Seats covered with black velvet and cushions so plump a person bounced slightly when they sat their bottom down upon it. Small tables for refreshments and snacks sat in between the seats and a smartly dressed footman stood at attention, ready to serve the slightest whim of the box's occupants. The view of the theatre stage was sublime, Ada was close enough to see the detailing on the set design.

The Treffaser's box sat a little to the left of centre and all around them, members of the aristocracy occupied their own boxes, munching on fruit and nuts and chatting quietly amongst themselves as they waited for the play to start. But a single large box, smack in the centre of all the others, in prime position, sat empty. It seemed a terrible waste. Theatre boxes were frightfully difficult to get, and very expensive. Why didn't the owner of the grand central box rent it out? Was it reserved for royalty?

"Is that where the Prince Regent or Queen Charlotte sit when they attend?" asked Ada to Aunt Caroline.

Aunt Caroline glanced at the grand box. "Oh, yes, I suppose the Queen and Prince do often accept invitations to sit there. But that isn't their box. It belongs to the Duke of Aberlay. Not that he uses it much. It's often the Dowager Duchess who sits there. Obviously, she isn't here tonight."

"Why not?" asked Ada.

"Tomorrow is the Aberlay ball, dear. It is only the most anticipated social event of the season. The Duchess will be busy with final preparations for that. No matter how organised one is, there is always something last minute for these things. And while I'm sure Her Grace employs a good housekeeper, there is only so much servants can do."

Ada stopped listening after the first sentence. She'd forgotten about the Aberlay ball. This would be one social event that Kit couldn't avoid. Her heart started pounding faster and she couldn't help the thrill of anticipation that shot through her. She was only going to talk to him, she told herself firmly. It was all one-sided anyway. Kit with his perfect, aristocratic features and lean muscular frame was leagues above Ada in appearance alone. But even if he had been squat and ugly, he still wouldn't have considered her. Dukes didn't marry ugly women. Or even plain-faced ones.

Not for the first time, Ada wished she had been born beautiful like Hetty. Then, maybe, the man she loved could love her back.

Ada glanced over at Mr Mellford. Sensing her stare, he turned and grinned at her, following with an awkward wave. Ada forced herself to smile and nod in response. It was one thing to marry a man you didn't love, another thing altogether to be in love with one man and marry another. But what choice did she have? Remain an eternal spinster with no children or home to call her own? And eventually when Mama and Papa died, she would go live with Hetty and Ashbourne, or some other relative who would take her. When all her youth faded, her hair turned white, and her hands gnarled with age, would she look back at this time with regret? Knowing deep down, she'd made the wrong choice.

The play began with an operatic flourish, the lead actor prancing onto the stage, demanding all attention. But as everyone in the audience turned their gazes forward, Ada's eyes remained fixed on the Duke of Aberlay's empty box. She found she couldn't look away.

Chapter 14
The Aberlay Ball

Since her first foray into the London Season, Ada had attended the balls of many great Lords and Ladies. But all those extravagant events paled in comparison to the Aberlay ball. Four actual trees, painted gold, stood in the corners of the massive space, their branches hanging with small glass and silver lanterns that together emitted so much light, the effect was dazzling, as if the tree itself was aflame.

Several stalls had been set up on the sides to dispense with all manner of snacks - fruit, nuts, cold meats, salad, sweets. And the beverages available were just as grand. Expensive tea, coffee and champagne flowed as readily into cups as lemonade or wine. It was all in such excess that it shamed any host who ever moderated their guests' consumption. Jugglers and magicians, garbed in finery, walked amongst the guests, performing their tricks for delighted ladies and cynical gents.

Already couples were dancing. Rich skirts swishing in time to the orchestra's full performance. Had she thought the ton dressed well before? Tonight they positively glittered, the dressmakers of London no doubt receiving huge quantities of business from this ball. But amongst all the finely dressed figures, there was still no sign of the Duke.

As soon as she'd arrived, Ada scanned the room in vain. Surely he would attend his own ball? Lord Buelle had danced a set with her, and then scandalously danced a set with his own wife. Mellford had claimed the waltz which Ada fastidiously pencilled into her dance card. Lord Wooten, an Irish Baron, came to collect her for the current set. Ada acted out the motions of the country dance, bowing and then raising her arms for the adjacent couple to skip through, all the while keeping an eye fixed on the entrance. And then, *he* walked in.

Every female under the age of fifty turned to look at the Duke of Aberlay, like flowers turning to face the sun. Ada was no different, as helpless to his draw as everyone else. The dark, striking features, the masculine energy he emitted so nonchalantly from the long stride of his legs to the broad lines of his chest. Just like his guests, he spared no expense in his dress and the sight of him took Ada's breath away. Tan buckskin breeches hugged the muscles of his thighs as intimately as any lover, the expensive evening coat clung to his broad shoulders and his white cravat, expertly tied, stopped just over the hollow of his neck, a place Ada desperately wanted to kiss. He locked eyes with her from across the room and all other men fell from existence. She went through the motions of the dance like some toy automation.

What Lord Wooten said to her, or she to him, Ada could scarcely recall. If she stumbled or stepped on toes, it was of no consequence. Everything in her body longed only to be done with this dance and close to Kit again. Her awareness followed him as he rounded the room, a flash of his dark hair behind the shoulders of a couple, the sound of his laugh as he passed an acquaintance, the fake polite one, not the deep sensual one Ada knew he was capable of when truly amused. Finally, finally, the dance came to an end and Lord Wooten led her to the edge of the floor. Kit ended his conversation and came to her almost immediately.

Her heart gave a pathetic little quiver before it started pounding furiously, and a sensation like pins and needles washed across the surface of her skin as her traitorous body flooded with desire no matter how much her brain tried to keep it in order. He stood within touching distance of her and no rational thought or command could keep every nerve ending in her body from singing at his mere proximity.

"Are you free for the next set?" he asked, eyes focused solely on her.

She had no idea. Ada nodded, her dance card lying forgotten and inconsequential on her arm in the face of Kit's undivided attention.

He took her hand in his firm grasp and led her to the centre of the floor. As the first strings of the song rang out, Ada caught a glimpse of Mr Mellford watching them with a vague expression of hurt on his face. Had she been supposed to stand with him for this dance? Was it the Waltz already? With the Duke's arms around her it was difficult to recollect who had claimed which number.

"Ada, keep your eyes on me," said Kit, his deep voice rumbling through her.

She turned her gaze to him and any fleeting concern for Mr Mellford was lost in the velvet blue of Kit's irises. There was no possibility of her looking away as she submerged under the spell Kit always seemed to be able to weave. His military body was equally suited to dancing as to fighting, the physicality of his male form at ease with any type of exertion and Ada only had to follow his lead as he led them masterfully through the dance's steps.

"You've been avoiding me," she said, and instantly regretted it. He owed her no explanation.

"After what happened last time, I had to stay away. I shouldn't have asked you to dance. I told myself I wouldn't."

"Because you're ashamed of me. You hate me," said Ada quietly, voicing her deepest hurt despite her rational mind screaming at her to stop.

His face morphed into one of shock and when he spoke his voice was thick with emotion, "I am ashamed of myself. I hate myself! Never you, sweet Ada. How can you think that? I could sooner cut off my own arm than think poorly of you."

"After what we shared last time, you said it was a mistake. You regretted it."

"Because you are a lady! As a gentleman and a man of honour I should've had enough self-control to stop myself from kissing you, from touching you, from giving myself liberties that should only ever be your husband's. I came this close to ruining you completely. If it happened again, I don't think I could stop myself. Where you are concerned, I am not a man of honour. I am little more than a beast let out of its kennel."

"No beast could have made me feel as you did," she said. He twirled her and their bodies briefly pressed together. An electric current passed from Kit's body into hers. When they faced each other again, he held her closer than before and his hot breath brushed against her cheek like a caress.

"You speak like that because you are a complete innocent in the ways of men. You have no idea all the wicked acts I wish to perform on you, all the sordid things I have thought of us doing together. I imagine it every night before I sleep and every morning when I wake. Things that would embarrass a whore."

"You're trying to scare me, but it won't work."

"I'm trying to shock some sense into you. One of us should at least have some, and I've learnt already that it isn't going to be me."

"You forget, I was right there with you. When you kissed me, I kissed you back and when your hands were on my body, I touched you too. You say I am innocent, but I feel just as guilty as you!"

"Then I have corrupted you. There is nothing you need feel guilty for, the blame is all my own." His voice dropped. "Even now I am consumed with carnal thoughts of you. Thoughts that would make the devil himself turn their face in shame."

"Carnal thoughts are in my mind also," she said softly.

Kit swallowed hard. Ada watched greedily the bob of his Adam's apple, longed to put her tongue on it. His arms never left hers. It was the Waltz after all. Briefly she thought of Mr Mellford, but he was like a figure behind misted glass, difficult to visualise when Kit with all his magnetism stood before her.

He shook his head. "Why do you toy with me so," he hissed. "Am I just a person to wet your appetites and then you will spend your life with Mellford? Don't try and deny it. I know you've been seen almost exclusively with him this past week."

What was she supposed to say? Of course that was how it must be. All her fantasies, all her vivid desires for Kit would have to be put aside if she was to marry. She looked at him, her heart shattering in her chest. "I don't deny it," she said simply.

His face shuttered and suddenly instead of his open expression, she faced a blank mask. Anger, passion, desire, all gone. "Fine. If that's how you want it, meet me in the garden in ten minutes."

The final strains of the Waltz rang out, a high, forlorn note that carried long after the violinist put down his bow. Kit and Ada stood frozen in the last aching position of the dance for a moment and then he all but threw her away from him, sending a cursory nod at her that strained the bounds of politeness. She drifted away from him to the outer reaches of the ballroom, a ship whose crew had abandoned her and left her to the mercy of the tides. That was where Mr Mellford found her.

Mellford swallowed hard before opening and closing his mouth several times. Ada waited patiently, still engulfed in the turmoil from her contact with Kit.

"Miss Adeline, it is because I respect you and respect myself that I must speak," he said at last, uncharacteristically careful, measuring every word.

"Go on Mr Mellford," she said.

"His Grace, the Duke of Aberlay, and you. I read about it in the gossip rags of course, but, well, I hoped, foolishly, that it was only idle speculation. He is famous after all, and news of him sells papers." He paused, gathering his thoughts. "But now I see it with my own eyes. How the two of you fit together. A matching set."

"His Grace and I are friends," said Ada.

Mr Mellford smiled but his eyes were sad. "Being second place to any man is an uncomfortable feeling, even if that man is the Duke of Aberlay. I am a simple person. The intrigues of the ton are beyond me. If I offered marriage and you accepted, would you be able to put your feelings for him aside?"

She clearly had been less effective at hiding her emotions than she'd thought. It would be easy to agree. To allow Mellford to court her with the steady assurance that after a brief period they would marry and Ada would have the pleasant home life she'd always desired, complete with a kindly husband, children and a house in the country. Mellford was also well off enough that there would be London seasons and carriages and new ballgowns; it was already more than Ada had hoped to have.

And if she still kept a place for Kit deep in the recesses of her heart that no man could ever touch, well, no one needed to know, certainly not her husband. She could hide it well enough that Mellford would never suspect it. In time, Kit would find an appropriate lady to make his Duchess, his path would diverge further still from Ada's. She would see him at the occasional ball or social function and smile politely while her heart twinged with its old longing for a man she could never have.

She looked at Mellford's earnest face and found she could not do it. She would've been a good wife to him, by the standards of most ton marriages, kind and affectionate and true, but she could not promise him premier position in her heart, not when Kit had claimed it so thoroughly for himself.

Mentally Ada shook her head at herself. Here was the perfect chance for a good match, one that Ada might never get again, and she was about to turn it down for a man so unattainable he might as well be the moon.

Ada spoke slowly, considering every word. The last thing she wanted was to cause more pain than necessary. "Mr Mellford, you are a wonderful man, and any woman would be lucky to have you as a husband. However, I do not think in good conscience that I can be that woman for you."

He nodded and swallowed hard. Despite her efforts, she could see that she'd still hurt him. Hopefully it was only his pride she'd injured, and his recovery would be swift. "I think a part of me knew for a while that the Duke had your affections, but I wanted to believe otherwise," he said, looking unhappily away.

Other than Hetty, who was now married and gone, there was no one for Ada to confide in about Kit, and she found herself being more honest with Mr Mellford than perhaps was strictly proper. "If it is any consolation to you, the Duke doesn't hold me in the same regard. So you see, we are both in the position of wanting someone who cannot feel the same way," she said.

"No, Miss Adeline, you and I are not in the same position at all. I suspect you will be receiving an offer of marriage from your Duke very soon."

She shook her head. "Our difference in rank is too great."

"You are the granddaughter of a Baron, that is not too low for a Duke, particularly one who is madly in love with you. Perhaps if he did not feel as he did, he would marry an heiress or the daughter of a peer instead, but such a small difference in rank will not stop him from following his desires in this matter."

"Mr Mellford, you say the most absurd things! The Duke is decidedly not in love with me."

"You need only see how he looks at you. It was foolish of me to try and come between that. You are a gem amongst women, and you deserve all the things that a man of his rank and abilities can give you. Besides, it is not such an embarrassing thing to be turned down by a future Duchess, clearly the competition was stiff."

It was extraordinarily flattering and demonstrably untrue. Ada didn't know what to say in reply, so she side-stepped it all together. "Let us stay friends Mr Mellford. I will always hold you in the highest regard."

"Thank you, Miss Adeline, I will hold you in high regard also, the highest regard. But I do not think I will make you a very good friend at present. Perhaps a better man could happily watch you marry someone else, but I need time to lick my wounds."

She had hurt him worse than she'd thought and that she regretted. "Very well, I shall await the day when we can be friends once more. And even if you cannot extend the same sentiment, I wish you every happiness that life can afford."

He bowed stiffly in her direction, and Ada watched him leave, a heavy feeling in her chest. Why couldn't she have loved Mellford? If she was more sensible, she could have just become very happy, and made a good man very happy as well. But neither reason nor sense seemed to rule in Ada's heart. There was only Kit for her, and because of that, she feared she would never be truly happy.

She thought of the Duke as he'd been moments ago and a treacherous wanting unfurled in her gut. He was waiting for her in the gardens. Ada should walk in the opposite direction. Gently bred ladies didn't meet men in dark, private settings. It would be confirming the accusation he'd flung at her last time, that she was a woman of loose morals. Maybe she was. After all, despite all propriety or good sense, her feet were already turning towards the double doors that led out into the garden and to the waiting Duke.

Chapter 15
A Denouement

She was barely a step on to the patio when a shadow separated from the wall. Kit. She would know his frame anywhere, even in the middle of the night. His hand encircled her arm and he dragged her forward and down onto the grass. The Aberlay's gardens were so vast that Ada had seen only a small portion of it during the Duchess's picnic. Now Kit led her down an unfamiliar path, past hedges and eerie marble statues, their forms barely distinguishable in the dark. They turned corners and rounded large trees, taking such a convoluted path that without him, she would be utterly lost. Her feet left grass to crunch across gravel, which eventually gave way to soft earth. They came to a stop before a wall of willow trees, their silver leaves trailing from the sky to the ground.

Kit swept back the leafy curtain and Ada gasped. A blue lagoon, previously hidden by the willows, revealed itself. The still water, mirror-like, reflected the full moon above. It looked like something from a dream scape or fairy story, the lake of Avalon from which Excalibur was given to King Arthur.

"Come," said Kit, taking her hand in his warm one and tugging her forward.

"Where? There's nowhere to go," said Ada. They were already at the edge of the lake.

"There's a path through," he said, and with his hand still holding hers, he stepped forward and was standing in the water itself. Ada looked more closely and saw Kit was actually standing on a small stepping stone, placed on the lake at regular intervals.

Ada followed him, the willow tree curtain closing behind her, shutting them off from the rest of the world. They leapt from stone to stone, Kit's steady grip keeping her safe from falling.

"Where are we going?" asked Ada, giggling when she almost slipped, but Kit's hand was there tugging her upright just in time.

He looked back at her with a grin, the first one of the night. The shadows of his face were deeper than ever in the darkness, the moonlight glinting off his eyes, and for a moment, Ada couldn't breathe. He looked like a faerie prince, full of mischief and magic. "You'll see. I used to come here all the time as a child. When my parents were arguing or just to think. It was somewhere I always felt safe."

And now he was sharing it with her. Ada felt the uncomfortable sensation of her heart being smashed into a pulp. This dear, beautiful man, whose parents had neglected him, who had all the responsibilities of such a great position thrust on his shoulders at too young an age. Despite all this, he still managed to be the most wonderful person she had ever known. She wished for just a second, just a moment of the day, that she could know what it was like to have her love returned.

That would be enough for her to be content with life. Even in this dark, hidden world she did not dare to imagine any more than that. The thought of Kit falling in love with her, not for a second, or for a day, but for the rest of his life glittered before her like a sparkling mirage, glimpsed for a second and then quickly swept away. Such a man would never love her, and Ada must be content with whatever time he shared with her, for it was sure to be brief and quickly forgotten on his end.

"Here it is," said Kit, startling Ada enough that she lost her balance. But no matter, even as she wobbled, Kit's strong arm wrapped around her waist and lifted her up and off the last stepping stone and onto dry land. She landed with both her hands on his hard chest and Ada got distracted by the heat radiating off him and the rich masculine scent of his skin.

She tore her gaze away from the hollow of his throat long enough to take in the small island they stood on. It was little more than a grassy mound, but at its centre stood a crumbling stone pavilion and the whole place, surrounded as it was by the silvery lake and the willow trees further out, took on the appearance of a place out of time.

"Kit, it's beautiful. Thank you for bringing me here," she said softly, because held like this in the circle of his arms, there was no need to speak louder than that.

"I've never brought another here," he said just as quietly, "but I wanted to bring you here, to see you in this place. You look just the way I imagined."

"How did you imagine I'd look?"

Kit fingered a tendril of her hair.

"Beautiful," he whispered, "You look beautiful."

And then he kissed her, his lips brushing against hers gently. Even as it was happening, Ada couldn't quite believe that it was. After he'd ignored her so thoroughly, that Kit would kiss her again, that she would feel his mouth move against hers like this, seemed so far beyond the realm of things that could happen in this world. Half thinking she must have slipped into some glorious dream she parted her lips and clung to him, threading eager fingers through the thick locks of his hair.

As if waiting for this, Kit groaned against her lips, and like a sudden torrent of rain the kiss turned hot and needy. He pressed her close until the hard length of his body was a heated wall against hers. Ada felt like she was melting, her body like a candle under a flame. It was all she could do to tilt her head back and hold him close as Kit plundered her mouth.

He kissed desperately at the corner of her lip and her cheek and then caught her earlobe between his teeth and tugged gently, "I've never wanted anything the way I want you," said Kit, his voice an octave lower than normal, his voice a husky growl.

"I want you too," whispered Ada.

Kit groaned and then his mouth was back on hers, silencing any further words with a lush kiss. She parted her lips almost immediately and shivered deliciously when for the first time she felt his tongue in her mouth, licking slow and purposefully in a way that had Ada's spine tingling. She arched into him, her body reacting in ways unfamiliar to her.

She was lifted into his arms and inside the pavilion before she even realised he was moving her.

"Kit?" she asked, finding her feet above the ground.

"There are pillows and blankets inside," he said and a second later he proved it by laying her gently down on the cushions scattered across the floor, "All stolen from garden furniture. I think the servants are genuinely worried about a thief in their midst."

The ceiling of the pavilion was open to the clear night sky and when Ada looked up it seemed like all the stars were shining tonight, a thousand tiny fairy lights. She giggled, delighted and aroused and feeling like she'd drunk too much champagne.

"You can't steal your own furniture," she said, smiling at Kit and feeling terribly fond.

He appeared above her then, his dear face more arresting than the night sky, his eyes seeming at that moment brighter than the moon could ever be. Ada stared at him transfixed.

"Why do I feel so guilty then?" said Kit ducking down to steal a kiss.

"Because you are too honourable. There is nothing to feel guilty about," said Ada, drawing him down for a proper kiss. That deliciously slow sweep of wet lips and the slick stroke of their tongues. He rolled slightly so that he was above her, his forearms on either side of her head and to have his long, hard body pressed against hers and his lips kissing her so thoroughly, it felt like she had captured the stars for herself.

In this secret world it felt as if none of her hidden desires were off limits. She trailed her fingertips down the hard planes of Kit's chest, feeling every heavy inhale and exhale he made, and then down to his waistband where she tugged his shirt out of his breeches and laid her palm flat on the bare skin of his lower abdomen. Kit shivered beneath her touch and he tore his mouth from hers, trailing hot kisses all across her jawline and down to the bodice of her dress.

One of his hands pushed up her dress and she felt his hot hand on the naked skin of her thigh, just above her stocking. Any part of Ada that concerned itself with propriety or rationality had long since fled and all that was left was a base animalistic creature. Her whole world was Kit, and at his touch she arched her back and parted her legs, wanting more, more of Kit, always.

His hand reached higher, the tips of his fingertips just brushing against the lips of her sex, while his mouth placed sucking kisses all across the exposed skin of her neck and chest. Mindless pleasure coursed through Ada, she dug her free hand into Kit's hair, tugging at the strands, urging him on. She wanted to touch him everywhere and when she slipped the edge of a fingertip into his breaches, Kit groaned and his hand came all the way up to cup her between her legs, the heel of his palm grinding slow circles into her sex.

Ada shivered, her hips moving against Kit's hand. She was making sounds she'd never made in her life, moans and gasps and little cries of pleasure, but she'd long lost control of her vocal cords along with the rest of her body. She could feel moisture between her legs, a gush of wetness and the hardness of Kit's body against hers felt like the only thing she'd ever wanted.

"Please, Kit, please," she cried, having no idea what she was pleading for but needing it desperately all the same.

"I know, darling, I'll give you what you need," he said, his voice hoarse. His clever fingers circled the nub between her legs, sending a sudden burst of pleasure through her, before trailing down to her entrance. Ada gasped when she felt the rough pad of Kit's fingertip pressing into her. She was so wet, the digit slid in easily. She stared wide-eyed at the sky above, overcome with pleasure, in shock that something could feel this good. Her core rippled around him, clenching and relaxing in a way that sent little shivers through her.

"God, you're so tight sweetheart, so goddamned perfect," he said, ripping his mouth away from her neck and sliding down her body. Ada thought she'd let Kit do anything he wanted as long as he kept using those endearments, every 'darling' and 'sweetheart' that fell from his lips echoing unendingly in her heart.

And then every thought fell straight out of Ada's head, replaced with white hot pleasure. Kit's head was between her legs, and his tongue, God, it was, Ada couldn't believe such a thing was possible, that he was licking her *there*, and sucking and then licking again, small little laps of his tongue followed by long, hard licks against her nub that had Ada screaming out in ecstasy.

At the same time, he slid another finger inside her, moving two digits in and out in a steady rhythm. Ada cried out hoarsely, clawing at Kit's scalp as the pleasure built inside her, her body writhed beneath him even as her hips thrust upwards into his hands and mouth. Between her legs Kit groaned and sucked harder like a parched man encountering water for the first time.

Every inch of her vibrated with pleasure and yet it still wasn't enough, she was desperate and aching for something. She had no idea what she craved but her animal brain knew it started and ended with Kit.

"Please, Kit, I need you," she whimpered, her entire body flushed and needy.

"God darling, I need you too." he said, dragging his head up. His lips glistened with her juices and when Ada stroked a thumb across his lower lip, Kit closed his eyes against it as if he was just as overcome by what they were doing.

Ada pulled him up, needing to kiss him. She stretched up, seeking his mouth with hers, finding he tasted like her when she slid her own tongue over his lips. Kit groaned into the kiss, collapsing onto her like a man possessed, stroking his tongue along hers.

One of his hands fumbled with his breeches and then Ada felt something hot and hard between her legs, resting just against her entrance. The realisation that this was Kit's manhood sent a wave of longing so startling through Ada that she gasped out loud with it, disconnecting their lips. She wanted him inside her so desperately, but the swollen tip of him stayed just outside in a maddening tease no matter how Ada arched her hips.

"Look at me, Ada," he said, the words sounding like they were wrenched out of him.

She opened her eyes to find Kit closer than ever before, his face tight with self-control. The pupils of his eyes had dilated almost completely so only a thin line of blue remained. Their gazes met and Ada couldn't look away. This Kit was nothing like the cold, composed Duke that graced the ballrooms of London, his dark hair was messy from where Ada had pulled and tugged at it and he looked like an animal barely restrained, lips bruised and swollen from their kisses, eyes wild around the edges.

"Ada, you have to tell me to stop," he pleaded hoarsely, "Tell me to stop, my love," he said again when Ada only stared at him.

It was those last words that broke Ada. My. Love. Spoken with such sincerity that for a brief, shining moment Ada believed it was true. She cupped his face in her palm and looking into those eyes that were so dear, she said the words that would damn them both.

"I need you."

Kit let out a small cry, sounding as if she'd mortally wounded him. And then slowly and inexorably the head of his cock slid past her entrance and into her pulsing core. They both groaned. It was just the tip, but already it was all encompassing. As Kit drove slowly forward, he met with resistance.

"I'm sorry darling, this will hurt for a moment," he said, pushing his hips forward in a rapid thrust.

It took a moment for Ada to register the pain, her body still attuned to pleasure. She whimpered, tears springing to her eyes. Kit kissed her through it, his lips pressing gently, almost apologetically against hers, distracting her from it.

After a while the pain faded, leaving only a sensation of fullness. Tendrils of pleasure grasped her once more and Ada found herself going lax, her legs falling apart as her body fully accepted Kit's presence inside her.

He began moving, slowly at first, an unending slide in and out that had Ada gasping against the cushions. Encouraged, Kit sank deeper, the force of his thrusts increasing. Ada's toes curled, her legs rising to wrap around him. The new position opened her up even further and they both cried out. Collapsing onto his elbows, he took her mouth in a searing kiss, his tongue playing with hers even as his hips kept up the devastating rocking rhythm below. Ada's sex clenched tight, skin flushed and tingling. Feeling wild and desperate, her hands twisted in his hair as her body began spasming with pleasure.

She shuddered, overwhelmed. Every nerve-ending alight as her body tipped over the edge into pure ecstasy. Her head thrashed and she cried out, breathless, as her core rippled around him and the world went white.

When she opened her eyes again, it was to see Kit, his beautiful face ravaged with pleasure. Between her legs, his thrusts grew erratic, barely sliding out before pumping back deep again. She held his gaze and watched him go over the edge, her own body still quivering as if in sympathetic pleasure. "Ada," he breathed, the sound like a prayer. She felt a spurt of hot liquid inside her and he cried out, body jerking, before collapsing over her, spent. Ada wrapped her arms around him, awestruck at what they had shared as Kit trembled through the aftershocks of his pleasure.

When he finally lifted himself up to look at her, it was with a stunned expression on his face. Slowly, as the remnants of pleasure faded from her body, Ada began to comprehend the seriousness of what she had done. *Ruin.* It was a word whispered amongst the ton when a lady disappeared to the countryside never to be seen again.

She who prided herself on being sensible, who'd admonished Hetty for the same sin, was now guilty herself. In one night, she'd not only rejected Mr Mellford, but also the possibility of any decent match for herself. All for a brief moment of bliss that would haunt her the rest of her life. Even now, while they were still connected, lying here in Kit's arms, the memory was tinged with the bittersweet knowledge that she had given herself in a one-sided act of love that was little more than a fling to the Duke. It was that last thought, that she meant nothing to him, that had tears springing to her eyes.

She looked away, trying to get them to stop, but they slid down her cheek regardless. Kit caught them with his fingertips, his expression morphing to one of concern. "Ada, look at me. This will all be well, I promise."

"You cannot promise that," she said, head tilted away.

"I can. I will." He gently nudged her face back to his and kissed her sweetly. It calmed her. When he helped her into an upright position, she blushed at her state of undress. But Kit gently put her together again, tugging her corset back into place, realigning the shoulders of her dress and smoothing back her hair. "Listen to me, this is what we will do. You'll go directly to your mother and tell her you are unwell and need to return home. I'll follow behind after a short interval."

He led her back across the stone steps, out of the lake, and being out of that magical place had the effect of sobering Ada up. "What do you intend to do?" she asked.

He looked at her, a sudden boyish grin on his face. "Marry you of course."

Chapter 16
What Honour Demands

The shock of Kit's extraordinary statement had worn off somewhat by the time Adeline reached home. Lady Deufont had whisked her youngest daughter away at the mere mention of illness. "The last thing you need is to be remembered as the debutant who sicked all over some gentleman's shoes." But that didn't mean her mother was pleased about it. All the way back, Mama vocally expressed her vexation that Ada hadn't danced with Mr Mellford. "That man is on the verge of proposing. You really must do everything you can to encourage him. And to think, you might be a Baroness one day. As things stand, Mellford is in line to inherit his uncle's title you know."

Ada did know. Her mother reminded her of it constantly. With a spurt of hysterical amusement she tried to imagine Mama's reaction at learning Ada was to marry far better than a possible Baron. The Duke of Aberlay was on his way here to make her an offer of marriage. The thought was shocking. In the darkness of the garden, he had just been Kit. But what he represented was far greater. The Duke of Aberlay. The highest title in the land, with all the accompanying veneration, wealth and grandeur. And he was going to make her his Duchess. Not because he particularly wanted to, but because in a moment of lust, she had trapped him. Ada sank to the floor of the entryway.

"Goodness. Stop talking her ears off about this Mullburn fellow," said Papa from the open door of his study, "Clearly Ada needs to rest."

"You do enough resting for this whole family," retorted Mama, and then more gently to Ada, "Can you get yourself into the parlour? I can summon a footman to carry you upstairs."

"No, please don't. I will be fine," said Ada, lifting herself off the ground and walking to the parlour where she gratefully sank onto the sofa. "I will go up in a moment."

Mama fluffed a cushion behind Ada's back and then her hands froze as she stared out the window. Ada turned her head. It was the Duke. His black carriage gleamed even in the darkness, the ornate Aberlay crest painted boldly on the side, declaring to all the family it belonged to. Mama's eyes narrowed. The Duke's part in Hetty's marriage was still on her mind. "What can His Grace want coming back here and at this late hour. Hasn't he caused enough disruption in this household already? I know he's a Duke but that doesn't give him the right to do whatever he pleases," said Mama.

From what Ada had seen, that was exactly what being a Duke enabled Kit to do. But she wisely kept her mouth shut. She didn't think she'd be able to speak anyway, even if she wanted to. She was so nervous that she began to feel ill in earnest. Muffled sounds came from the hallway. The slam of Papa's study door. Last time the Duke talked to Papa, both Mama and Ada had been asleep. This time, they were not.

Both Ada and Lady Duefont scurried across the hallway and pressed their ears against the door. Mama might resent the Duke for his part in Hetty's marriage, but she would still hang on to every word he said. Ada didn't particularly want her mother to hear the exchange between Kit and Papa, but there was no way to get rid of her. The voices of both men sounded clearly through the thin wooden panelling of the door.

"Your Grace, you'll forgive me if I don't stand. My leg is troubling me."

"Not at all Sir Walter."

There was a scrape of wood across the floor. The sound of Kit sitting in the armchair across from Papa's. Her father spoke first.

"Back again. I suppose you've come to petition for Ada's hand on behalf of some gentleman or the other. It can't be Hetty again as she's already wed. You saw to that. I must say though, it is highly unusual for a man of your station to take such an interest in the marital prospects of my daughters."

"Perhaps sir, if I tell you my purpose in coming here, you will not find it so strange. Indeed, I *am* here to petition for your youngest daughter's hand in marriage. But not for another gentleman. I seek Ada's hand for myself."

There was a crash and a muffled curse word from her father. If Ada had to guess, she'd say Sir Walter had fallen out of his chair. Next to her, Mama slapped a gloved hand over her mouth. A hushed gasp still slipped out, but probably not loud enough for the men to hear. Her mother gripped Ada's arm firmly with her other hand and looked at her daughter wide-eyed. Ada tried to shake her off, but her grip was too strong. She ignored whatever message her mother was trying to convey with her eyes and focused back on the conversation. From the sounds of it, Sir Walter had just regained the ability to speak. Although not very well.

"You. You want to marry Ada? My Ada? But. But. You're a Duke."

"Even Duke's get married, Sir."

"Yes, Yes, of course they do. But generally, not to the daughter of a Baronet. I mean there's nothing wrong with Ada. She's pretty enough, and her dowry is not insignificant. But you could have any woman in the ton. Any number of women with far more beauty and money."

"I'm not marrying Ada for money. I'm marrying her because I love her. A quality that is infinitely more precious to me than the fortunes of all the heiresses in England put together. Besides, I have plenty for both of us. I assure you, Ada will never want for anything financially. I intend to settle fifteen thousand a year on her for pin money. And she may have more from me if she requires."

Another gasp from Mama, and this time more audible. And no wonder. Even Ada was shocked by the sum. Fifteen thousand a year was more than triple the total amount her parents had to run their entire household. And Kit intended to settle this on her merely as pin money.

"And as to her beauty, I consider Ada more beautiful than any woman I know or will know. I must confess I am astonished to hear you say Ada is not as pretty as other women of the ton. She is widely considered this season's incomparable. My mother and Lady Jersey said so just the other day, and while my opinion may be clouded by my affection, they cannot be accused of the same."

"Well, I never. My Ada. This season's incomparable. And about to become a Duchess." Her father let out a laugh of astonishment. "I would never have guessed this. Lady Duefont was barking after the wrong daughter this entire time. I always did think there was something charming about Ada, something in her expression and the slant of her eyes. And now my little girl will be a Duchess." Another laugh of astonishment.

"Does that mean, Sir, that you give your permission?"

"Yes, of course, I could hardly refuse such an offer for my daughter. The final choice must be hers, but I will consider her a very stupid girl indeed if she turns down this chance."

"I do not think anyone who knows Ada could ever call her stupid." said Kit with a hint of coldness in his voice. He may be a man petitioning a father for his daughter's hand, but he was still a Duke. And Ada's heart thrilled to hear him standing up for her.

"No, yes, of course, I did not mean to imply. That is, welcome to the family my boy, uh, Your Grace. I will send for Ada at once."

"There is no need. I will address her in the parlour. With your permission," said Kit.

There was not even a question in her father's mind of Ada turning down the Duke. And indeed, as far as he was concerned, why would there be? This was the pinnacle of rank and status that any woman in England could hope to achieve. But Ada didn't have a choice. Circumstances had made it so that if Kit didn't marry her, she would be ruined. All the pleasures of being a Duchess paled in comparison to forcing the man she loved into a marriage he didn't want but felt honour bound to go through with.

Kit's chair scraped back, signalling the end of his conversation with Sir Walter. Mama jumped away from the door, and this time Ada was grateful for the grip on her arm because it pulled her away too and snapped her out of her thoughts. They both hurried back into the parlour and Ada had just sat down when Kit came through the door.

"Lady Duefont. I would like an audience with your daughter. In private."

Under normal circumstances there might have been some protest at leaving her unwed daughter alone with a red-blooded, young man, even if that man were a Duke. But clearly, her mother was willing to bend the rules given what was on offer. Ada tamped down a hysterical giggle, if only her mother knew that there was no longer any virtue left to protect.

Her mother got up and left silently, but not without a heavy glance in Ada's direction. The door closed, shutting them off from the rest of the house and Kit was beside Ada in a second, his long strides crossing the floor with ease.

Ada caught his arm and dragged him towards the window, the part of the parlour furthest away from the rest of the house. The room was a lot bigger than her father's study and this far away from the door and inner walls, there was little chance of being overheard no matter how Mama pressed her ears against the panels.

He stood a lot closer than he normally would and Ada was temporarily distracted by the sheer, male presence of him. She could smell the spicy scent of his hygiene products and when she tilted her head up, her mouth was just inches away from the underside of his jaw where a small, previously unnoticed scar sat to the left of his ear. It would be an easy thing to reach up slightly and press her lips to it.

"Your father has given his permission," said Kit, his voice low and quiet in deference to their closeness. There was no need to speak loudly, and his voice was so close to a whisper that it called to mind the things Kit had murmured into her ear when he had been inside her.

"Kit, I don't want you to marry me."

Kit visibly stiffened and he moved a step away. Ada braced herself and continued, "You are being trapped into a marriage you don't want. Perhaps

I'm not with child after all, the likelihood is that I'm not. We could wait and see. If I'm not, there is no reason for you to marry me."

Kit's face went blank and she couldn't tell what he was thinking. He grabbed her suddenly, forcing her to look at him. "There is every reason for us to marry. Don't you understand? I've had you. I've taken your virtue. I've claimed you in the way only a husband should. Would you marry another man, knowing that I've already had that part of you, that before him you'd already given yourself to me?"

Ada shivered, remembering how thoroughly Kit had indeed claimed the rights of a husband. She could still feel him inside her. There hadn't been time to clean herself and she was still slightly sore and moist between her legs with the juices of their lovemaking. She squeezed her thighs together, but that only heightened the sensations.

"Would it be so terrible to be married to me?" he asked softly.

Tears came to Ada's eyes, sudden and unwanted. She blinked them away angrily. There was a horrible, selfish part of her that wanted nothing more than to marry Kit, even if it meant entrapping him. Even if he kept mistresses and later fell in love with some of them, he would only ever have one wife, her. She would hold a place in his life reserved for no other woman, and she wanted desperately to take anything and everything he could offer her, even if his offer fell short of love.

"It wouldn't be terrible at all," she said, her voice horribly choked up.

"Oh Ada, darling, it will be wonderful. You'll see. I'll make it wonderful." It was said with such quiet sincerity that Ada didn't have the heart to dissuade him. How could she tell him that she didn't care for pin money, or jewels or endless parties. What she wanted was for him to feel as she did.

So, when he cupped her face in his hands and brought his head down slowly for a kiss, Ada tilted her head up and slipped her arms around his neck. She might as well enjoy her deal with the devil. The heartache would come later, when Kit no longer touched her so delicately or swept his lips across hers so carefully because he was getting that somewhere else.

The kiss was tentative, as slow and gentle as their first. It lacked the heat of their earlier lovemaking, but it was exactly what Ada needed. This kiss felt like a promise, it spoke of loyalty and devotion, and it calmed Ada even as it slowly rekindled the old flames that had settled into embers. It would just take a slight tilting of Kit's head or a brush of his tongue to turn the kiss into something heated and desperate, but he refrained, kissing her so softly that Ada felt like a bowl of butter melting in the morning sun.

She mimicked his movements, the slightest press of lips, the briefest meeting of their mouths as they shared a hundred small kisses that melded into a long, continuous one. She could feel herself clinging to him, holding his head close to hers so that it wouldn't stop. Without the burning heat that normally dictated their embraces, there was no distraction from the feelings rampaging through her heart. The kiss felt like her soul was being sucked out of her body.

There was a knock on the door, loud and insistent enough to cut through the thick, syrupy feelings Ada was wrapped up in. Kit jumped away, putting a respectable distance between them. Just in time, as Mama bustled through the door, her face turned expectantly towards Ada.

"Well?" she said, after a long moment of silence.

Ada cleared her throat. "His Grace has made me an offer of marriage and I have accepted."

Her mother squealed, loud and high in a way that Ada had never heard before in her life. She practically bounced across the room, sweeping Ada up into a tight embrace. "Oh, my dear, what wonderful news. Why, I couldn't be happier."

This was more enthusiasm than her mother had ever shown and Ada bore it as best she could, wrapping her own arms gingerly around her mother's waist. Over Mama's shoulder, she locked eyes with Kit. His dark gaze fixed upon hers and for a moment the world fell away as she slipped once more into the spell between them both.

It was Kit's turn to clear his throat. Ada noticed his lips looked as swollen as hers felt. They must have been kissing a long time, she thought hazily. At the sound, Mama let go of Ada and turned to the Duke. "Oh, Your Grace, my heartfelt congratulations to you too! How happy you shall both be."

Kit bowed in Lady Duefont's direction, "By your leave, I will go directly to my own mother and inform her of my impending nuptials. I am sure she will be in touch. The Dowager Duchess will no doubt want to assist with the preparations."

Between her mother and Kit's mother, Ada doubted she would be required to do any planning for her wedding. Kit bowed again, this time to her and his eyes softened, "Until next time, Miss Adeline."

Ada watched him go until his coat tails disappeared behind the door frame and there was nothing of him left to see. Beside her, Mama was nattering away in an excited fashion. "Think of all the dresses and jewels, the parties in London. My daughter, a Duchess, the leader of the fashionable set. The most famous woman in England. There won't be a single door closed to us. Oh, how wonderful it will be to see people and tell them casually, 'my daughter, the Duchess of Aberlay'. I always said that you must have a London Season and look at the result!"

In fact, her mother had implied many times that Hetty was the one who should have a London Season and that the expense was likely wasted on Ada as she wouldn't marry any better for it. And Ada had believed her, internalising the message that she wasn't beautiful enough for a great match, that she needed to settle for less. Now she was engaged to the most sought-after bachelor in the land. But he was marrying her out of obligation, not desire, and she was just as unattractive as always. Ada suddenly felt exhausted, a wave of tiredness hitting her all at once along with the beginnings of a headache. It would be just typical if she were to fall ill after all.

"It's been a long day, Mama, if it's alright, I'm going to go to bed."

"Yes of course dear, and you feeling poorly as well." Mama sighed, clasping her hands together. "Why the Duke must have fallen in love with you at that very ball and come directly here. How romantic. How wonderful."

Whatever else her mother might have said was lost as Ada left the parlour and climbed the stairs to her room. Blanche was waiting up for her, which lightened her heart. With Hetty gone, the room they had shared seemed too empty. She missed her sister's happy chattering, and tonight more than ever she felt the keen loss of her sibling. If there was one person she could have safely shared her emotions with, it was Hetty. Hetty would neither judge nor reveal Ada's secrets. But Hetty was on her honeymoon, and so when Blanche smiled eagerly at her, Ada plastered a smile onto her face in return.

"Oh, Miss Ada, is it true? Are you to be a Duchess? All the servants are whispering it."

How quickly news travelled. It would seem that events had barely transpired upstairs before it was common knowledge in the kitchens. "Indeed, it is," said Ada, "The Duke of Aberlay made me an offer and I have accepted it."

"Oh, bless me! My mistress a Duchess! That is of course, I mean, a great lady such as yourself will probably be wanting a more experienced lady's maid."

"Don't be silly Blanche. Of course, I shall take you with me."

"Oh, Miss Adeline, thank you. I'll do you proud, you'll see. I promise I'll learn everything there is to learn. I'll be the best lady's maid a woman could have. Well, I'd better be if I'm going to serve a Duchess," said Blanche excitedly as she stripped Ada of her dress and combed out her hair. It seemed everyone else was far more enthusiastic about Ada's marriage than she was.

With the night's jewellery carefully put back into its cases, Blanche reached for Ada's undergarments, but Ada waved her away. "Thank you, Blanche, I'll do the rest myself. It's been a late night for you too, and I'm sure you want to get some sleep."

"But Miss Ada, it's mighty tricky to get the laces of a corset undone, let me help you. It won't take long at all."

"No Blanche, I'd like to be left alone now if you don't mind. I need to compose my thoughts. It's been quite a day." She gave her maid a reassuring smile, "I'll call you back if I really can't get it off, but I'm sure I'll manage. Thank you, Blanche."

"Of course, Miss Ada," said Blanche, dropping a quick curtsey and leaving with Ada's dress to be cleaned and ironed in the morning.

Adeline waited until Blanche's steps disappeared from the landing, then she got up and locked the door. No matter how hard it was to get her corset and chemise off, there was no way Ada could get any help with it. A single glance between her legs would reveal everything she and Kit had done tonight. And there was no way gossip this salacious wouldn't spread across the entire town, jumping from house to house as virulently as a plague. Blanche wouldn't mean it to, she would tell just one close friend and then that friend would tell another very close friend, and before long every person in London would hear of it.

Unfortunately, this was one of those corsets that laced at the back. Ada tilted the mirror on her dresser at an angle so she could see the fastenings in the larger, standing mirror. Luckily Blanche never tied the strings very tight and a few tugs at the base and the top had them loosened enough to slip the contraption up and over her head.

The chemise was far easier, without the support of the corset it slipped off easily, falling to a silken puddle at Ada's feet. She was left standing in her stockings which only reached up to mid-thigh, held in place by the garters. Between her legs was smeared the clear, thick liquid she'd sometimes seen from her own body, but in far greater quantities than ever before. And more tellingly white patches of Kit's seed and a tiny smear of dried blood presented indisputable evidence of what they'd done.

Grabbing a hand mirror and a washcloth, Ada gently wiped first the inside of her thighs and then parting her inner lips with two fingers, she cleaned around her quim. It was still highly sensitive, and she hissed at even the most delicate of contact. The cotton of the washcloth felt unbearably rough, even though she knew it wasn't really since she'd used it on her arms and neck before. After all the mess was wiped away, Ada continued staring between her legs. She'd never really looked at herself like this.

It was odd that Kit was now more familiar with this part of her body than she was. Ada stared in fascination at the pink lips and the little bud nestled in between them. That was the part Kit had put his tongue on and sucked. Tracing two fingers further down, she felt the opening where Kit had entered her. Despite her fastidious attentions, she was still moist there, though it was nowhere near how wet she'd been when Kit had been touching her. Her entire sex looked pink and a little swollen, but there was nothing now to indicate that she was a woman who'd lost her virtue, only her memory of the act.

Hetty had been right after all. Even though it sounded odd and uncomfortable, actually doing it had been wonderful. The difficulty had come afterwards, when the weight of what the act meant came shoving rudely into reality. Ada was sure that a major reason for how good it felt was Kit. It may have been just as unpleasant as she'd imagined it with any other man, but with him it had felt like the most intimate and natural thing she would ever do. It occurred to her with a sense of wonder, that once they were married, they could do it again and again without any consequences. And they would have to do it again, because Kit needed the legitimate heirs that only a wife could give him.

That was something at least, thought Ada, as she pulled on her nightdress and snuggled under the covers. To be the mother of Kit's children and his companion in the eyes of the world wasn't nothing. And she knew whatever Kit might feel, he would always treat her honourably, he was that kind of man. Really, if Ada hadn't done the vastly stupid thing of falling in love with him, it would all be fine, more than fine.

With Hetty gone, there was no one to see the tears slide down Ada's cheeks or hear the quiet sobs she muffled with her pillow. She really was a very silly, very stupid girl. And ungrateful too. The Duke had given her everything that a debutante could ever want, his name, his title, wealth beyond belief. She and any children they had would never want for anything. And he was so kind, and noble and lovely in just about every way. So why could Ada not stop sobbing?

Chapter 17
Wedding Jitters

White's gentlemen's club was thick with cigar smoke as it so often was this time of evening. The haze and general darkness of the room affording Kit a degree of anonymity. He nursed a whiskey as he regarded the portrait of King George on the wall. Perhaps Kit could join him in his madness. He took a long swig, feeling it burn down his throat.

He had never wanted a marriage like his parents. A marriage made of duty, seeking affection in the arms of others. But that was precisely what he'd foisted on Ada. She didn't want to marry him. She loved Mellford. The thought made him want to smash his whiskey glass across White's hardwood floors. Instead he took another sip, not bothering to savour the expensive beverage. But no matter how much he drank, he couldn't shake the wretched guilt over his actions.

She had been a perfect innocent. And he'd taken that from her. He remembered clearly the moment when he'd pushed past her virgin barrier, that brief resistance giving way to his brutish attentions. When he'd shoved his cock in her. God. Nothing in his life had given him so much pleasure. He'd been like an animal, all instinct, stripped of any human reason, grunting and panting above her, overcome with need. And innocent, beautiful Ada, not realising what he was doing, had clung to him, holding him in her arms as he destroyed her world. Of course she wouldn't think to stop it, it was on him as a gentleman to protect her virtue. And she had trusted him, which made the offence worse.

He should never have let it get that far. Never even told her to meet him in the gardens. He'd only intended to kiss her one last time before she married Mellford. Which was bad in itself. But jealousy and a deep longing had led him inexorably from one thing to the next. A brief kiss grew languid and intimate, developed into heavy fondling and before he knew it he was between her legs. His tightly wound control gone.

The worst part of it all was that when reason returned after his mind-melting orgasm, it was not guilt but triumph that struck him first. He'd stolen Ada from Mellford and any other man who might hope to have her, and a wicked, selfish part of him had delighted in it. Of course, the irony being that even though she would be his wife, he wouldn't stop her from becoming Mellford's mistress. No matter how much he wanted to, he wouldn't stand in the way, though it would kill him to watch Ada go to another man's bed. For his part, he would remain faithful to her. It was the least he could do.

"You should put some ice in that. Your head will thank you tomorrow."

Kit looked up to see his friend, Viscount Manderville.

"I'd rather not remember anything tomorrow."

"Ah. In that case forget I said anything about the ice. What's the unhappy occasion?" asked Manderville, sinking into the armchair beside Kit and pouring himself a scotch.

"I'm engaged to be married."

"Congratulations. Normally that is cause for celebration, not this sad state I find you in. What's the matter? Is she an ogre? A dull companion? Missing a limb? You can surely work around that last one."

"No. She's lovely in every way," sighed Kit.

"Ah, so the woman in question is Miss Adeline Duefont then. My God Kit, I would've thought you'd be delighted. I'm delighted for you. This is the woman you practically confessed your love for last night."

"She doesn't love me. She's in love with Mellford."

"She told you this?"

Kit nodded morosely. "She was set to marry him."

"But she isn't. She's marrying you. That's got to mean something. If she really loved Mellford, I don't think any amount of titles or wealth would sway her. She chose you," said Manderville.

"That's just it. There wasn't a choice. Not for her, not for me, not after…" he trailed off, unable to voice it, but Manderville understood at once. Of course he did. Unlike Kit, Manderville had always been careful to never tur a debutante. His friend's expression grew soft. Kit turned away from him.

He didn't want pity.

"Look Kit, love can be something that grows slowly. Not everyone feels it immediately. If she doesn't love you now, she very likely will in the future. Lady Sarah Caser didn't care for her husband when she wed, now she adores him."

"And yet she still tumbles into bed with you regularly," said Kit.

"Perhaps not the best example. What about Lord and Lady Carmichael? If the rumours are to be believed they hated each other on their wedding day. Now they live in marital bliss."

"Because they both keep separate households and hardly see each other," said Kit. He buried his face in his hands. "God, I'm going to have a miserable marriage, aren't I?"

"No wait, all right, I'll admit there aren't many examples amongst the ton, and the two I picked were particularly bad as examples go. Ah, look, your cousin Sir Henry is coming this way. He was happily married I think?"

Kit looked up from his hands to regard the older man, a distant cousin from the Aberlay branch. Sir Henry was well into middle-age but still handsome. As a young man, he'd made his fortune in the military, then entered politics as an MP in the House of Commons. He could have easily remarried, but it showed a remarkable devotion to his dead wife that he had not. Instead the man had raised the sole child of their union all by himself. By all accounts his young cousin Jane was growing up to be quite a forthright character, but he'd expect nothing less from Sir Henry's daughter.

"I understand congratulations are in order my boy!" said Sir Henry, thumping Kit on the back so hard the whiskey threatened to slosh out of his glass.

"It's barely been a day. How did you find out so quickly?" asked Kit.

"Jane called on Marianne earlier. Anyway, all of London will know soon. She tells me your mother has written to the newspapers. It'll likely be on the front pages of The Times tomorrow morning."

"You better get used to everyone congratulating you then Kit," said

Manderville, "It'll be inescapable for a week at least."

"I'll elope," said Kit.

Sir Henry laughed. It hadn't been a joke. Kit was seriously contemplating it. "Don't worry old boy, it'll be worth it in the end. Most debutantes are

insufferable creatures, but your Miss Adeline is exceedingly lovely. I met her at some ball or the other and she made quite an impression. You've chosen well. I imagine you'll be very happy together."

"Were you happy in your marriage?" asked Kit. It was a personal question, but he was too drunk to care.

A sad smile broke over the man's face. "For the brief time I had her in my life, my Eleanor made me happier than I ever thought possible. Even with all the grief that came with her passing, I wouldn't trade it for the world."

Now Kit felt like an oaf. Bringing up Sir Henry's dead wife was tactless in the extreme, and it was clear that the remembrance of her still brought sorrow to his cousin's heart. But it was proof of what Kit had suspected but never had evidence for, that marriage, done right, could be truly blissful. "You must share a toast with me, Sir Henry. That I will find some of the happiness you did in my own marriage."

"I'll drink to that," said Sir Henry agreeably, pouring a scotch for himself. Manderville needed no incentive to drink.

"To a happy marriage," they chorused.

Kit drank deeply. He needed it.

Ada had, at least nominally, been wedding planning for the last few days. In reality, there was very little for her to do except smile, nod and try to be a neutral arbitrator between her mother and the Dowager Duchess of Aberlay. The two matrons seemed to have the wedding planning firmly in hand, the Dowager Duchess perhaps more so than Mama.

The shock of Ada's engagement had barely sunk in, before the Dowager Duchess was at their door, arriving so early the next morning that the household was still eating breakfast. Leaving her eggs half eaten, Lady

Duefont received her in the parlour and quickly discovered that she would have far less say than she'd imagined when it came to planning Ada's wedding. The Duchess had arrived with firm ideas from everything to the colour of the napkins at the reception to the member of the clergy that was to marry the happy couple. And in order to ensure it could all be done by the date she had decided for the wedding, it was accompanied by a strict schedule crammed with back-to-back appointments.

"Well, we can organise the bans to be read in Riverstoke immediately and then set the wedding three weeks later," Ada's mother would say.

"Bans? Absolutely not! The Duke of Aberlay will be married with nothing less than a special licence a week from now," was the Dowager Duchess's reply.

"The local vicar would be very happy to perform the ceremony?" offered Lady Deufont tentatively.

"The Archbishop of Canterbury will perform the ceremony. He is a close friend."

"Lilies for Ada's bouquet and the church flowers," said Mama.

"Lilies always remind me of funerals," said the Dowager Duchess, "Roses are better."

They both turned to look at Ada in unison. "Perhaps we could have both?" she ventured.

"An exorbitant expense," cried Mama.

"Money is no issue," said the Duchess firmly, putting a firm tick in her notebook beside both flowers, "Kit has told me we have an open purse in this matter. Whatever Ada wants."

Ada ducked her head to hide her blush, but it was unnecessary. They'd moved onto hymns which was a hotly contested subject and neither Mama nor the Duchess were paying attention to her. Ada dozed off slightly when they began debating the individual stanzas of 'Joy to the World'. She hadn't gotten much sleep lately and the room was warm and her armchair soft.

A hand shook her slightly, and Ada startled awake. It was the Dowager Duchess, looking down at her with an indulgent smile.

"I was just closing my eyes," said Ada.

"I understand. It's been a busy time and you likely have had little sleep," said the Duchess, "I'm sorry to wake you, I just have something to give you before I go."

She held out a large velvet box. A jewellery box. The clasp was a tiny version of the Aberlay crest. Ada popped it open and lifted the lid. Inside was the most exquisite diamond set she'd seen in her life. Not even Queen Charlotte's diamonds had glittered so finely. Each stone on the necklace would be the centrepiece of any other ornament, but here they all glittered together like tiny stars, reflecting the sunlight into thousands of tiny beams. Nestled beside the necklace were other pieces, each a work of art on their own. A cluster of diamonds made up two earrings, and a bracelet not to be outdone, was set with a double row of the stones.

"The Aberlay diamonds," said the Dowager Duchess at the look of awe on Ada's face. "Exquisite aren't they? I've seen many expensive jewels in my life around the necks of princesses and queens, but never any that could rival these. They belong to the Duchess of Aberlay. So now, they are yours."

She touched the edge of an earring with trembling fingers. How could these belong to her? And yet, here was the Duchess, handing them over, expecting Ada to accept them. "Thank you," she said at last, taking the box tentatively.

"My dear, you'd better get used to being the recipient of expensive gifts. My son will bestow many on you."

But as the days passed there was no sign of the Duke, let alone any gifts. Ada could not help feel this was a sign of his regard. Or rather, lack of regard. An absent fiancé as a precursor to an absent spouse.

Chapter 18
In Sickness and in Health

The morning of Ada's wedding was all a beautiful blur. The sun was bright, the air unseasonably warm, the Aberlay diamonds around her neck sat cold against her skin, a constant reminder of who she was marrying, despite his absence. If Kit had just visited once since his proposal, Ada wouldn't feel so terrible. But the engagement felt like a signal for how their marriage would be.

Ada was no fool. Kit had proposed because his sense of duty compelled him to. And although her husband was an honourable man, Ada knew how marriages in the ton worked. Great men, unless incredibly devoted to their spouse, kept mistresses. And those women were the recipients of the love and affection they didn't feel for their wives.

If she'd married Mellford, he likely wouldn't keep a town mistress. But Kit was one of the wealthiest men in England, and a Duke besides. Not to mention far more handsome. He could easily keep a dozen paramours in unimaginable luxury and visit a different one each night. There would even be married women of the ton who'd jump at the chance to share his bed. The thought made her sick with grief and helpless anger. But there was nothing to be done except swallow it down. She understood the deal. He gave her the protection of his name and title and all the privileges that went with it, but she wouldn't have his love. She would have to satisfy herself with his occasional visits and in time, if she was so blessed, the company of their children.

The church was cold when Ada entered to the sounds of organ music and choral singing. She was dimly aware of the lavish decorations in her periphery, but it all faded rapidly in importance. Kit stood before the altar, rigid in his military uniform, more handsome than any man Ada had ever seen. Greedily her eyes passed over the width of his shoulders down to his narrow waist and then back up to his penetrating gaze which she met with a shock.

He was examining her just as closely and Ada blushed at the attention, hoping she passed inspection. She knew she looked better than she ever had today. And yet, compared to him, she felt woefully inadequate. Like someone had dressed a pig in the garb of a Duchess. Expensive silks, flowers, diamonds, but underneath was still a common creature, unworthy of marrying this man.

Ada gratefully placed her cold hand into Kit's large, warm one as they both turned to face the altar together. The Archbishop droned on about the duties of marriage and then it was Kit's turn to speak his part in the ceremony. Ada listened with a heavy heart as he spoke pledges to her he had no intention of keeping.

"I, James Bartholomew Ruthmoore, take thee Adeline Mary Duefont to my wedded wife, to have and to hold from this day forward, for better for worse, for richer for poorer, in sickness and in health, to love and to cherish, till death us do part, according to God's holy ordinance."

His strong voice reverberated around the church, each word sounding so sincere that for a brief, shining moment, Ada was able to convince herself that he meant everything he said. But as the last echoes of his voice faded, so did this belief.

With a shaky voice, she spoke her own oaths. The words themselves gave her strength. Even if Kit did not keep to his vows, she would keep hers to him. To lie with another man, feeling how she felt, would injure some deep part of her. By the time she got to "till death do us part," her voice rang clear and true around the church, pledging her life to Kit before the gathered witnesses.

Compared to the glittering diamonds she'd been presented with earlier in the week, the ring he slipped on to her finger was incredibly plain. Ada didn't think it was gold, or even silver. From the dull grey colour, she would guess steel or iron, an odd choice for a wedding ring, particularly for a wealthy Duke. Ada hoped it wasn't a sign of his esteem, that a wife was so far down his list of priorities that any old junk from his treasury would do.

They knelt together and when the Archbishop bade them rise, it was done. How odd that less than an hour could change one's life so drastically. It took mere moments for a woman to be ruined, and then, mere moments to become engaged. And in the same short space of time to go from plain 'Miss Adeline Duefont' to 'Her Grace, the Duchess of Aberlay', a title with so much weight and gravitas Ada could practically feel it settle on her shoulders as the priest announced them to the congregation.

They left the church and entered the waiting carriage, Ada sneaking glances at Kit. He was staring resolutely forward as if determined to avoid her. Ada's heart sank in her chest. Would they pass the entire ride in silence? He made no move to speak, so Ada resolved to go first.

"Are we going directly to Wolsley?" she asked. The ancestral seat of the Aberlays was familiar to anyone with even a passing knowledge of England's great stately homes and was regularly visited by scores of people. Ada even before knowing Kit, had always wanted to see Wolsley.

"No. I cannot be away from parliament for long. I've sent word for an estate in Kent to be prepared for our arrival."

"Ah," said Ada. Silence descended once more. The rattle of carriage wheels across cobblestones the only sound. Ada adjusted a fold of her dress. "And how long are we staying?" she ventured again.

"Three days. Including travel time."

Ada's heart sank. Half a day's travel each way meant only two days really. That was all the time her husband wished to spend with her. Hetty and Ashbourne were taking months. But Ashbourne loved Hetty.

They didn't speak again. Not until the carriage rolled to a stop outside a massive manor house, and Kit had led her up the stairs. The servants, after an initial greeting, made themselves scarce. After all, this was supposed to be a wedding night. Even if her silent husband showed no interest in it. They paused on the landing.

"The housekeeper has prepared the Duchess's chambers for your arrival, if you would prefer to spend the night there," said Kit.

Ada searched his face. Did he really wish for her to go and sleep in another bed? It was the only part of their marriage Ada had felt she could rely on. That night when she and Kit, in their passion, disregarded the rules of society. It had, despite the consequences, felt so natural. The thought of spending her wedding night away from him sat poorly in Ada's stomach. But he had already sacrificed so much for her sake. If that was what he wanted, she wouldn't object.

"I am sure the Duchess's chambers will be very comfortable," she said carefully.

Another pause.

"My chambers are also very comfortable," he said at last.

Ada's heart rate picked up. "Perhaps even more comfortable than the Duchess's chambers?" she asked.

"We'll have to try them both to decide. Shall we start with the Duke's?"

"It's as good a place as any to start," agreed Ada.

He led her into a room bright with candles and the orange glow of a well-lit fire. A large four-poster bed dominated the room, the silk curtains drawn back to reveal its soft bedding. It was big enough for Kit and Ada and about three other people to sleep between them.

Kit closed the door behind them. They were alone, no possibility of interruption. Apart from the sizzle of the fire and Ada's own breathing the room was silent. Both embarrassment and desire intermingled within her. Kit looked at her steadily, heat in his eyes, and Ada felt that heat drawing her in, causing a corresponding reaction in her own body.

He reached for her, thickening the thrum of passion between them, his large hand folding around the nape of her neck and drawing her slowly and inexorably towards him. Ada slid eager hands under his jacket and across the broad, warm expanse of Kit's chest, tilting her head up in anticipation of his kiss as desire bloomed within her. *Yes*, her mind cried. This was what she'd craved through days of Kit's silence.

Soft, firm lips brushed against hers, more a gentle tease than a proper kiss. Ada shivered. She parted her lips and he pressed in gently, mouth moving against hers slow and syrupy. It was much steadier, much more careful than last time when the passion had exploded between them in a flurry of grasping limbs and hot, animalistic kisses. Ada found herself gliding into this arousal more slowly, her mind still intact enough to register Kit's careful ministrations and take stock of the way her body responded to his.

The way the slow glide of his lips sent nerve endings tingling. The way her breasts felt tender and heavy, pressed up against Kit's chest, and most delicious of all, the slowly blooming heat between her legs. Her whole body yearned for his in a way she hadn't understood the first time he'd taken her. But now she knew the shape of what was between them, knew that before the night was out, Kit would be inside her in the most intimate way imaginable and the knowledge sent her pulse quickening and her lips parting in encouragement.

But Kit would not be hurried. No matter how she scraped her fingernails through his silky, black hair or rubbed her lithe figure against his, he continued those painstakingly unhurried kisses until Ada was all but clawing at him in desperation.

"Kit please," she pleaded at last, pulling her mouth away.

His eyes glittered with hunger, but also with determination. "No Ada, I'm going to treat you right this time. The way I should have before. We're going to do this properly."

She bit her lower lip in frustration and the motion drew his gaze, impossibly his eyes darkened further and Ada felt sure this was the end of any kind of measured approach. He would take her in his arms and kiss her and touch her and handle her with the same explosive lust as the first time. But Kit closed his eyes and drew a shuddering breath and when he looked at her again she saw that his determination had conquered his hunger.

He took her gloved hand and slowly, drawing the fabric away from her fingers, he kissed each inch of newly exposed skin before letting the glove drop discarded to the floor. Lastly, he raised her now bare hand and placed a tender kiss on the centre of her palm. He repeated the gesture on her other hand and then circled around behind her so that his clever fingers could slowly undo the tiny buttons that ran the length of her wedding dress.

"You make an excellent lady's maid," she said with a nervous laugh. This was so different from last time. Kit had never undressed her before and the gentle care he was taking with her garments made her feel suddenly vulnerable.

He pressed his lips to the back of her neck and then tugged her earlobe gently between his teeth as if unable to help himself. Ada shuddered deliciously in response. "Would you hire me, Ada? What would be my duties besides dressing and undressing you, which I'm already proving adept at," he said with a tug on her gown that sent it pooling to the floor.

Ada stood in her thin chemise, corset and stockings. For a moment Kit's arms encircled around her waist and she leaned back into his hard figure as he dropped his head to lay scattered kisses across her neck and newly exposed shoulders.

"Well, I would ask you about your hair styling credentials," she said.

"Not very good I'm afraid, unless just rolled out of bed after hours of lovemaking is the look you're going for."

The words, 'hours of lovemaking' whispered in her ear sent a shivery delight through her that hardened her nipples and had her insides clenching and unclenching.

"Well, never mind," said Ada, "Perhaps you are more talented when it comes to the sewing and repairing of clothes."

Kit shook his head against the nape of her neck before he reached down to undo the laces of her corset, loosening the fastenings with slow, steady hands. "I cannot sew either, unless you count rough military stitches. Nothing good enough for the clothes of a Duchess."

"That's a shame," said Ada as the corset dropped to her feet, "Are you skilled in any areas other than the undressing of ladies?"

"When it comes to the duties of a lady's maid, I'm afraid not. But you'll agree that my undressing skills are very good indeed," he said, releasing Ada from his arms and returning to face her again. She felt the loss of contact keenly.

He kneeled before her and lifted Ada's stockinged foot onto his knee. The slit in her chemise parted obligingly to give him access to her upper thigh and his large hands smoothed over her calf, behind her knee and up to the silk garter that sat only inches away from her hot core. Fingertips glanced over the soft, bare skin of her inner thigh as he tugged down the circular fabric that kept her stockings in place.

Again soft kisses rained down on every exposed inch of flesh, Kit's lips pressing against the sensitive skin over her knees, against her calf, against the hollow where her ankle met her foot. He was worshipping parts of her body Ada had never even thought about and they responded to him, goosebumps appearing wherever Kit's lips made contact with her skin.

Both stockings removed, Kit looked up at her, his unblinking eyes raking over every inch of her body possessively. Even though he was the one on the floor, Ada had never felt so aware of the power and masculinity of him, of the barely contained restless energy and the intensity of his want. Her chemise did nothing to conceal the poke of her hardened nipples, darkened with desire and clearly visible through the thin, white cloth and if that was not enough of a sign of Ada's arousal for him, the fabric between her legs had grown wet with her juices during Kit's ministrations, turning it transparent where it stuck so closely to the shape of her mons and nether lips that Kit didn't even need to remove the chemise to see her sex.

Last time, her chemise had stayed on, along with most of her other clothing. But this time, even her most inner garment would not be spared. Kit rose, pulling the last layer up with him and over her head. She stood naked before him, the first time Ada had ever been naked for a man. Though she knew as her husband, Kit had the right, self-consciousness still leaked in, especially when, apart from his discarded jacket, he stood fully clothed before her. She folded her arms across her breasts.

His hands, warm and gentle, clasped each of her palms and slowly drew her arms out and away, exposing her to his sight once more. She flushed but allowed him to look.

"You never need to be embarrassed about anything we do here Ada. You're mine to look at, to touch, to hold, and I'm yours too."

"Then let me look at you," she said with a determined tilt of her chin.

Kit nodded and then swallowed hard. Ada followed the bob of his Adam's apple with hot eyes. Then his fingers were at his throat, tugging his cravat out, undoing the line of buttons on his shirt. Unlike his careful undressing of Ada, his hands were clumsy on himself. He fumbled on the fastenings, failing to undo buttons on the first attempt. It was reassuring, a sign that she wasn't the only one affected by this.

When he reached for the buttons on his breeches, Ada's breath caught. Last time she hadn't been able to see between his legs, their midnight fumbling hadn't allowed any time for looking, only for the feel of him entering her.

A line of dark hair trailed down from his abdomen and as he pulled down his breeches and pantaloons she saw that the dark hair continued into short wiry curls against which his member stood to attention, long, thick and flushed red with blood. It was topped with a mushroomed head, almost purple in colour, with a single white bead of liquid at the top. Ada had never seen anything so arousing in her life. She wanted to run her fingers down it, feel the weight of it in her palm and taste the liquid leaking out the head.

He kicked the last items of his clothing away and stood before her naked, making no moves to hide himself, though he trembled slightly under her gaze. He was shockingly beautiful, so blatantly masculine in every way. Broad shoulders tapered down to a chiselled chest and abdomen. Ada had touched him through his shirt enough to know the skin there would be hot and rock hard. She found herself breathing in short panting gasps as she looked at him, her heart beating faster with the arousal quickening in her veins.

The dark locks atop his head matched the dark hair between his legs and served to draw her attention to his manhood jutting proudly towards her. In a way, he was even more exposed than her, Ada's sex was hidden between her legs, whereas his was out in the open, completely and unavoidably exposed to her gaze.

"I've never done this before," said Kit, his voice an octave deeper than usual, an underlying tremor to it.

"You've been with women before," said Ada.

"Not like this. I've never undressed for a woman, never let her look at me the way you're looking."

Ada frowned, "How can you have been with a woman without undressing?"

"The way we did it last time. Just flap open my breeches and plough into her. Sometimes the woman undresses, most of the time not.

"The way we did it last time. You could have left me, not given me your name."

"Never. I could have never done that to you."

He came forward and crushed his mouth to hers briefly before lifting her into his arms and walking the few steps to the bed. Ada buried her face in his neck, breathing deeply the rich, spicy scent that clung to his skin. He laid her down on the soft bedding gently, and blanketed her body with his, taking her mouth again.

Ada's hands wandered greedily over his body, scraping through his hair, smoothing over his waist. Her legs tangled with his, the soft skin of her calf rubbing against the rough hair of his leg. Kit's fingers stroked possessively over her body, as his tongue plundered her mouth, until at last his seeking digits dove between her legs, finding Ada wet and swollen, sensitive to the slightest touch. She gasped out loud, breaking their kiss and Kit took the opportunity to turn his lips on her neck, her shoulders, travelling down her navel with his mouth until his head was at her mound.

Sure fingers parted the slick folds of Ada's sex and then Kit licked firmly at her clit, sending Ada arching off the bed as electric pleasure shot through her. She buried her fingers in the silk of his hair, clawing when he swirled his tongue skilfully over her throbbing nub. His fingers quested lower still, circling her entrance. Ada was so wet, that two digits slid in easily and she thrust her hips up to meet Kit's hand, suddenly desperate to be filled with him.

Ada moaned. "Please Kit. I need you. Don't torture me like this."

"I was under the impression I was the one being tortured," said Kit, his hot breath over her sensitive sex sending Ada clenching around his fingers.

"Then put an end to it," she cried. "Give us what we both want!"

For a moment she thought he would deny her and continue his merciless teasing. But then, his eyes went dark and he hissed, "*Yes,*" a single word that drew another moan out of Ada. Kit took his manhood in his palm, and Ada watched him greedily. He was big, and she didn't think it wrong to think that the sight of it was beautiful, devastatingly arousing. He eased slowly into her and Ada whimpered, parting her legs further to accommodate that girth.

It was not the first time and they were married. Pain and shame had no place here, only pure, undiluted pleasure. Ada arched and clawed at Kit as he buried himself fully inside her, squeezing her inner muscles around the delicious weight of him. Had she ever felt so complete? Kit held himself above her, forearms straining, his tense body sheened in a layer of sweat, muscles gleaming in the golden firelight. He was looking straight at her, eyes wide as if he couldn't quite believe how good it felt. Ada reached up and dragged him down, craving his skin everywhere. He buried his face in the crook of her neck, a muffled 'Ada' said with the groan of a dying man and then he was thrusting into her, short, sharp movements of his hips that sent all thought flying from Ada's head.

Afterwards there was no hurried redressing, no sickening sense of guilt or despair, no garden to flee from. Instead their naked bodies lay entwined in the sheets, breathing deeply. Kit got up to fetch a cloth and Ada felt his absence for only a moment before he was there again, wiping the fluids of their lovemaking off her body, dropping fleeting kisses across each patch of newly cleaned skin. He gathered her into his arms and Ada fell asleep to the sound of Kit's heartbeat.

Chapter 19
Honeymoon Days

The Eldsmere estate in Kent was grander than any place Ada had ever lived and it was still considered small by Ducal standards. She walked past rooms with Grecian pillars and elaborate cornices and marvelled at architectural flourishes.

"And this is the parlour, Your Grace," said the Housekeeper. All morning it had been 'Your Grace' this and 'Your Grace' that, the title and accompanying tone of deference still new and surprising. The elderly woman swung open a wide set of double doors to reveal a sunny room upholstered in the finest pale pinks and blues. "It was decorated in the French style by the Duke's late grandmother, the third Duchess of Aberlay."

"Did you know her?" asked Ada,

"No, I did not have the pleasure, but that is her portrait there above the fireplace."

An austere woman in Georgian attire looked down at them. Ada wondered if beneath the powdered wig was the same dark Aberlay hair she'd twined through her fingers as Kit had kissed her this morning.

"She was a Duke's daughter herself," continued the housekeeper, "I believe it was an arranged marriage. Neither she nor the then Duke were particularly happy in it. How much better it is to marry for love," finished the housekeeper with a smile towards Ada.

Most everyone thought the Duke had married her for love. After all, what other reason could he have? Ada certainly was not the daughter of a Duke, nor was her dowry particularly impressive by the standards of the ton. Every time someone alluded to their great love match, it filled Ada with a degree of shame and embarrassment. The necessity of Kit marrying her had prevented him from finding love in marriage. She hoped he wouldn't resent her for it.

"Is there a portrait of the Duke in the house," asked Ada. Although they had spent the night together, he had dashed off on estate business in the morning and Ada found she already missed the sight of him. How much worse would it be when he left her more permanently?

The housekeeper frowned. "No, I don't believe so. But there is one of the late Duke, His Grace's father, in the next room. There is a great likeness between the two."

The Housekeeper had not lied. The imposing figure of the last Aberlay Duke stared down at her as if mildly disapproving of her union with his son. Ada stared back curiously. Kit's father had the same dark hair, the same arrogant tilt of the chin, the aristocratic nose. But Ada did not think she was being too biased in thinking that of the two, Kit was the more handsome. There was something about the openness of Kit's eyes, the shape of his mouth, a slight difference in bone structure that taken together made him devastatingly handsome in a way his father was not.

"It's a good likeness. I've seen him many times. He would come down a lot from London, where His Grace spent most of the year."

"And does the son come here as frequently?" asked Ada.

"I can't say he does. His Grace spends more time in the primary Ducal seat. As it should be. Not that that is a criticism of the late Duke, I would never speak badly of the Aberlay family." There was horror in her tone as if speaking ill of the Aberlays was akin to speaking ill of God.

Ada waved off the housekeeper's explanation. "Please don't trouble yourself. I know exactly what you mean. Now, I haven't seen the orangery yet, I understand it looks onto the apple orchard?"

Kit happened upon them inspecting a miniature banana tree. "I imagined a plant could excite so much interest." Ada turned at his deep voice, her heart rate picking up as she greedily drank in the sight of him. Their gazes locked, a knowing smile playing at the corners of her husband's lips.

Beside her, the housekeeper flung into a deep curtsey and then excused herself, bustling away with a knowing glance in their direction. No doubt she was going straight to the kitchens to gossip about her master and mistress.

Once they were alone, Kit moved closer. Close enough that she could smell the scent of his aftershave.

"How is the tour going?" asked Kit, reaching out to tuck a curl of Ada's hair behind her ear. Her pulse thudded at the casual intimacy.

"It was going very well until a certain Duke interrupted and scared my guide away."

"Ah, my apologies then. Is there any way I can possibly make it up to you? I am forever at your service."

If only that were true. "I'm not sure. How do you propose to make it up to me?"

"Hmm," said Kit, "I could buy you expensive jewels. A diamond for every indiscretion?"

Ada shook her head.

"Dresses then. Finest silks from the orient. Imported just for you."

She shook her head again.

"What would you like then my exacting mistress? All my fortune is at your disposal."

"You may keep your fortune if you tell me something. Something you've never told anyone else."

"Like a secret?" he asked.

"Yes, but more than that. A truth about yourself that no one else knows."

Kit paused. He led her out through the glass doors and they walked the grounds of Eldsmere in silence. The carefully cut lawn with sculptures placed at strategic intervals made for pleasing surroundings. Ada, content to wait for her husband to draw his thoughts, wondered if he would fob her off with a joke, some light-hearted tale that would amuse but not reveal anything real.

At last he spoke. "I'm proud."

"Kit, that's hardly-"

He interrupted Ada's protest. "Yes I know you'll say that's not even a secret, let alone a great unknown truth. But if you'll hear me out."

Ada closed her mouth and nodded, allowing it.

He drew a breath. "When I was eighteen I went to University and for the first time had a semblance of freedom. Until that moment, my father had been a distant figure to me. Someone who I thought loved and admired me from afar. On my first free day, I decided I would go to London and surprise him. In my naivety, I imagined he would be happy to see his only son. The reality was very different."

Ada's heart broke as she imagined a young Kit at eighteen, not yet the man he was today, seeking his father's approval. Being rebuffed. She put her hand over his, entwining their fingers. "What happened?"

"My father informed me in no uncertain terms that I was only the continuation of his legacy. My place wasn't to question him. I was his duty and nothing more. He held no love for me, not really."

"Oh Kit, I'm so sorry."

"The reason I went to war wasn't some great nobleness of spirit or a desire to serve my country. I only went to spite my father. It was pride that drove me to it. I didn't want to be part of his legacy. That is my secret. I am not the selfless hero people imagine, just a boy who hated his father."

"It sounds like you were justified in doing so. No son should hear what you did from his father. I saw his portrait today," said Ada, "You look a lot like him."

A flash of anger passed across Kit's face. "I hope that is where the resemblance ends. He was cold and performative in his duties. With minimal affection for those he should care most about. His only concern regarding me was how I reflected back on him."

In his words was a world of pain. For all Ada was overlooked and harangued by her mother, she'd never gotten the impression that she wasn't loved by her. If anything, her fussing suggested the opposite. This was altogether different.

Gently, Ada cupped his face in her palm and turned him to face her. His eye's were open and vulnerable and all she wanted to do was shield him from the suffering of the world. She could not, so instead she pulled him down and kissed him. Trying to convey all the affection and care she felt for him in her heart.

Kit was quick to bring his arms around her, crushing her to him and deepening the kiss immediately. His lips were hot against hers, deep, searing kisses that contained an edge of desperation to them.

When they broke away his lips were red. She brushed her fingers over them and smiled when he nibbled on her fingertips.
"You're far more than the Aberlay legacy. You're my husband. A good, noble man of character. And I'm so proud of you. Not because you are a

Duke and have fancy titles but because of who you are, who you have become despite your father."

Kit smiled. "You are a good wife to me, my Ada."

"It has only been a day. I think you should give it a little more time before deciding that," she teased.

"No, no, I'm quite sure. I'm certain the assessment will be the same whether we've had a day of marriage or years of it."

She laughed. "I'll certainly endeavour to make it so. Tell me, what qualities would you say make for a good wife?"

"Hmm," he said, pretending to consider the question. "She must have dark hair, deep blue eyes, a rosebud mouth that I could kiss all day, a small freckle under her left eye."

She laughed realising he was describing her exactly. "Be serious Kit."

"Alright, I suppose she is kind, sweet, a little tart sometimes. Teases me, but never in a cruel way, is understanding, thoughtful, in short someone I could happily spend the rest of my life with."

Ada's heart pounded harder in her chest. It almost felt as if Kit could be talking about her. But no, theirs was a marriage of necessity. She would do well to remember that.

"Speaking of tart things, I've arranged for lunch in the pavilion. It looks down into the valley below and since it is a fine day, I thought you might enjoy the view."

He led them to a round stone structure on the grounds of the estate, in which a small table with garden chairs sat facing outwards. Industrious servants had left a veritable buffet of food out.

She sat down, mouth watering. The Kent countryside stretched out before Ada, just as Kit had promised. Sheep grazed on green fields interspersed with hedgerows and small creeks. Everything was pastoral, peaceful.

"I wasn't sure what you'd like so there is a little of everything. Cold meats, fruit, pastries, cheeses, some pies."

"I hope you haven't been running the household ragged preparing all this for me? I don't want them to resent their new mistress straight out the gate."

"On the contrary, they are happy to have work for once," said Kit, sitting down beside her and reaching for an apple slice.

She snorted. "That's what they tell you at least. Besides, I'm sure taking care of such a large estate is plenty of work already. I don't know how you manage to keep track of them all. It seems unbelievable that this is just one of many."

"Good estate managers are worth their weight in gold," said Kit. "I was lucky to inherit most of them along with the properties. I don't consider myself particularly astute at land management, but I've made small expansions and innovations to the estates that will hopefully increase their value for the next generation."

"Our children."

"Yes," he agreed with a smile, "Our children will be dazzlingly rich."

His eyes slid to her stomach and Ada felt her breath pick up.

"There could be a child in me even now," she said quietly.

His eyes darted up and locked with hers, gaze heated.

"It could have happened the first time I had you," he said just as softly.

"Or last night," she said.

He reached out and traced her jawline, tipping her chin up with his fingertips. Ada arched into the kiss, pressing her upper body against Kit's.

He groaned. "Ada, you must eat."

"Suddenly I am not so hungry for food."

"You must keep up your energy. I intend our afternoon to be quite vigorous."
She leaned back and popped a cube of cheese in her mouth, watching Kit under her lashes the whole time. He stared back, lips slightly parted.

"In that case, you must eat too. Not just stare at me."

He swallowed and then reached for a pastry, biting into it and chewing rapidly.

"I'm thinking now that lunch at the pavilion was a terrible idea," said Kit.

"Oh, why is that? I'm rather enjoying the view," said Ada, eyes still on Kit.

He snorted. "I think the view would have been equally enjoyable from somewhere much closer to our bedroom. Dragging you back to bed will take so much longer now."

Ada laughed. "There are bound to be some initial problems in a new marriage. Picking the wrong place for lunch is a forgivable offence."

"You may forgive me, but I don't think I can forgive myself," he said with a dark look at her.

She looked around. "You know, apart from the sheep, I think we are quite alone."

Ada blushed at her forwardness, but the way Kit's eyes dilated couldn't allow her to regret it.

"My sweet, daring little wife. If you'll permit me, I'll sup on something far more delicious than anything the best cooks could make."

It was midday, broad daylight. Any passing servant or groundskeeper could happen upon them. But when Kit knelt before her and slowly rucked up her skirts, Ada did nothing to stop him. She didn't stop him when he kissed hotly up her thighs, or when he gently parted her netherlips, most damningly of all, she made no protest whatsoever when he licked sinfully into her core.

"Kit," she cried out, clutching at him. His answering moan reverberated through her.

Clever fingers slipped inside her wet entrance, thrusting slowly, mimicking their coupling. His mouth stayed fixed on her nub, lapping and then drawing tight little circles with his tongue before sucking gently. "Don't stop," she gasped, her fingers raking through his hair as her whole body trembled in pleasure. She arched into his mouth, hips thrusting up against her will.

He brought her to shuddering completion twice before fumbling with his breeches and entering her in one endless thrust. They groaned together as Ada clenched around him. Kit began a sharp, relentless pace, moving in and out of her. His hands clamped around her hips, repositioning her so that he was penetrating deeper than ever before. The new angle reached places inside her that no one ever had before. She gasped, spasming about him as that familiar wave of ecstasy flooded her body.

Kit let out a guttural sound. He kissed her, sloppy now. His hips thrust into her, once, twice and then he was calling out her name and trembling as his body succumbed to the same pleasure he'd so skilfully wrought in Ada. They clung to each other, panting like galloping horses as their heartbeats slowly returned to a normal pace.

'I think we may have scandalised those sheep,' whispered Ada.

Kit lifted his head to follow her gaze. A couple of sheep were indeed looking in their direction, their unblinking eyes vaguely judgemental. Kit laughed. "We'd better ensconce ourselves in our bedrooms for the remainder of our time in Kent. I wouldn't want to offend the delicate sensibilities of our cattle."

'You'll get no objection from me," agreed Ada.

Chapter 20
London Again

Ada's worries about a short honeymoon proved to be entirely unfounded. Whatever Kit may feel for her, since that first wedding night, there had been no decrease in passion between them. Even now, back in London with all its demands on their time, they could barely keep their hands off each other. And they had not spent a single night apart. Lying now as they were in the Ducal bedroom of Kit's London house, Ada felt that she had never been so happy in her life.

She traced the faint scar across Kit's lips with her fingertips, then down his chin to the underside of his jaw. Another faint scar slashed white across the skin where his neck met his shoulder. Here she pressed a tender kiss, thanking God the wound hadn't gone deeper and deprived her of her husband.

"You could have been killed," she whispered. Generally, men joined the military to make their fortune, accepting risk to life for the rewards. But not Kit. He'd stood to inherit one of the richest dukedoms in England.

He swallowed, and she felt the bob of his throat against her lips. "I was young, and like most young men, I thought myself immortal. Death would happen to other people. Not to me." Kit shivered as Ada's mouth brushed against his nipple, his arm tightening around her. "My first serious wound burst that illusion quite quickly."

"Where was the first one?" she asked.

"Here," said Kit, reaching down to touch his waist, where a red, puckered starburst ruined the tanned smoothness of the skin there. "A bayonet that went a little too deep. I was lucky it missed my organs. Or so they told me. remember feeling distinctly unlucky at the time."

Ada reached down to kiss over the poorly healed wound, tracing the edges of the scar with her tongue. Beneath her Kit inhaled deeply, his hands reaching down to wind themselves in her hair.

"My father was furious of course," he continued, his voice vibrating up from his chest and into Ada from where she was pressed against him.

She rested her chin on his abdomen and looked up, "You were his only son."

"He was concerned he'd lose the heir to his Dukedom. All that concerned him was duty. Duty to his rank and position to marry appropriately and raise an heir. He didn't love me. That was made clear when I found him playing house with his mistress."

Ada's whole body froze up. This was a new detail. "Oh," she said.

Kit sighed, ignorant of Ada's inner turmoil, he stroked his hand through her hair, running his finger through the tresses. "I remember my father's long absences as a child. At the time, I thought it was down to the demands of the Dukedom. But later it all made sense. When he died, I saw the receipts, cold financial proof of where his true regard lay. Gift showered upon her, far more than he'd ever spent on my mother. And more than money, she had the gift of his time. Where he could have been with his wife and children, he instead spent months at a stretch with her."

Ada's heart hurt. Was Kit laying out her own future? Stuck in one of the Dukedom's many country estates with only the servants' pity for company, while her husband whiled away his years in the arms of a mistress.

"Your poor mother," she said.

"You needn't feel sorry for her. She went into the marriage with her eyes wide open. She knew her husband didn't love her, and she was willing to make that bargain for the prize of being a Duchess. It wasn't long before she was leading society. I think she could have made his life very difficult if she'd wanted to. But despite the lack of love, there was respect and understanding between them. In their way, they were friends I think. That is the best most marriages of the ton can hope for."

Was that what Kit expected from her? To be like his mother. Respectful of Kit, understanding of his mistresses, friendly with him outwardly, despite dying inside with love for him. Tears welled up in Ada's eyes. How could she do it? Smile and be polite, knowing that the same night, Kit would be slaking his lust in another woman, sharing with her his body and his heart.

"I suppose most lords keep mistresses," she said, unable to keep the tremor from her voice.

"Ada, what's wrong?" Kit asked, realising at last some of her emotional turmoil. He sat up to see her face, and it was his look of gentle concern that tipped Ada over the edge, from sadness to sudden anger. What right had he to look at her with such tenderness when he was likely already planning to leave her for another woman. Lying lazily in bed with Kit, caressing his body as if she were really his lover was suddenly unbearable.

She ripped herself off him, reaching blindly for her robe and tied it hastily around her body as if it would provide some protection from her pain. He stood too but made no move to cover his nakedness. Head to toe, the very picture of male perfection, his muscles still glistening in a sheen of sweat from their love making. The thought of another woman seeing him made her feel sick with jealousy, and that loosened her tongue.

"I suppose you will be keeping a mistress as well. After all, you are a Duke. In fact, why limit yourself to one? Why not a dozen? One for every month of the year you will be ignoring your wife."

"I have no intention of ignoring you Ada," he said. Instead of angry, he looked pleased, as if Ada's emotions were of no consequence, a smile playing on those lips she'd kissed only moments ago. His reaction inflamed her fury further, even as a part of her was distantly aware that her outburst was likely to drive him away faster.

"No? You will be perfectly polite I suppose? How did you put it? Understanding, respectful and friendly while you *fuck* other woman on the side." It was a word Ada had never used before in her life, knew of it only days before through Kit, and yet it came to her tongue perfectly as if waiting for this moment.

"My, such dirty language for a lady. Why seek company elsewhere if I can find such filth at home," said Kit, closing the distance between them so that Ada was looking up at him.

Ada felt abruptly embarrassed, but still she was unwilling to relinquish the anger. "It's a word I learned from you. No doubt one your mistress will use freely."

"You seem very caught up in this idea of me keeping a mistress," he said softly, pushing Ada's hair out of her face and cupping her cheek in his palm, "Ask me not to have one if that is what you want."

"What?"

"Ask me for what you want Ada. You will find there is very little I will deny you."

A tremor started through Ada. How could she ask him for that? She had no right to stop him seeking love in another. And yet she wanted his faithfulness desperately. Desperately enough to ask even if she was going to be rebuffed.

"Ask," he prompted again.

Ada met his eyes with defiance, finding them soft and gazing down at her with a strange expression. "I don't want you to take a mistress. Ever."

There. She said it. She waited for his rebuttal and her humiliation.

"Agreed. No mistresses. Ever. What else?" he said.

Ada stared at him wide-eyed, disbelieving, a sudden sharp joy in her chest. He was waiting for an answer, but she had none.

"Will it be acceptable to sleep with other women as long as I don't keep them as a mistress? Can I take lovers among the married women of the ton, or seek out common prostitutes at Covent Gardens?"

She paled. Of course it had meant little to agree to no mistresses. Her husband wouldn't need to keep a woman for sexual favours. One look at him, and women rich and poor would leap at the opportunity to bed him.

"No other women. Ever," she whispered, too scared of her request to give the words a normal volume.

But Kit standing so close, caught them perfectly, his eyes on her making it impossible to look away. "Yes. Agreed. No other women. Ever. As long as I live, there will only be you Ada. You shall be the only woman to see me unclothed, the only woman I spill my seed in, the only woman I spend the night sleeping beside. No mistresses, no concubines, no unhappily married women of the ton, only you. You have my perfect fidelity. Does that satisfy the green-eyed monster of jealousy within you?"

She nodded, shocked at what he'd agreed.

"Then come back to bed," he said, untying her robe with deft fingers and slipping the garment off her shoulders. It dropped to Ada's feet in a puddle of silk and when he pulled her back towards his heat she melted against him readily.

Ada clung to him as he laid her horizontally, his powerful body blanketing hers as Kit covered her body in biting kisses and tantalising swirls of his hot tongue. The knowledge that his body was hers and no one else's soothed the insecurities that lay deep within Ada, and she found herself freer with her touch than ever.

Running greedy fingers down the planes of his hard chest, she cupped him boldly, feeling the heated length of him jerk in her palm. "God Ada," he muttered, his head dropping as his hips thrust involuntarily against her grip, "you could get me off just like this and it would still be better than with anyone else. Your slightest touch is enough -" he dropped off into a moan, as Ada curled two fingers around his crown, rubbing at the slit where moisture was beginning to gather, the precursor to Kit's release.

"Sweetheart. The things you do to me." His voice was low with desire, sending a shiver through Ada. "You have to stop, I'm too close," he implored, his eyes shut tight as if trying to block out the pleasure of it. He buried his face in her shoulder, and Ada clutched at his head, pressing him to her.

Kit's fingers, normally so clever, shook as they parted the folds of her cleft. He moaned at finding her already wet for him. "I love how easily your body readies itself for me, look how greedy you are, already trying to suck me inside."

She gasped, arching as Kit slid just the head of his cock into her. Already, her walls were convulsing trying to bring him deeper. "Kit. Stop teasing me," she begged behind gritted teeth, as he held himself inches away from what she wanted.

"If I asked, would you become my mistress?" he said, looking down at her writhing beneath him. Sweat glittered on his brow, and his face was tight with desire, but he still held himself away. "Do you want me so badly that you would consent to have me any way you could, even if I couldn't offer you titles or wealth? Only dishonour?"

Ada was too far gone to guard her words. All she could think of in that moment was the perfect satisfaction of Kit thrusting deep into her and stroking those hidden places only he could find. "Yes. Yes, of course I would," she cried, "Didn't I already? I wanted you so badly I let you ruin me. I would've become a ruined woman for you."

'And if I were a poor man? A farm hand or a milliner. Would you want me then?"

Desperate Ada cried, "Yes. Yes, please Kit. A thousand times yes. I'd want you always, no matter the circumstances."

At last Kit moved his hips, a slow, endless thrust inside that had them both gasping out loud with how good it was. This was what she needed. Ada wrapped her legs around his narrow hips, determined not to let him tease her again. But Kit was done with teasing. Gripping her knee, he held her open as he rocked into her over and over, setting a punishing rhythm that had Ada exhaling in a series of moans.

The slap of skin against skin, the intoxicating scent of their lovemaking and their shared gasps and cries of pleasure filled the room. Kit brought them both to the cusp of completion over and over until Ada's body was one unending lightning rod of pleasure and Kit was the only thing her senses could perceive.

"Ada!" Kit snarled out at last, his beautiful features contorted with pleasure. His muscles trembled as the movement of his hips grew erratic. He was falling apart in her arms. And the knowledge that it was Ada who'd made him this way had her shuddering as her own orgasm finally ripped through her.

Afterwards, they clung to each other and Ada fell asleep listening to the steady, reassuring beat of Kit's heart. Her last thought was that this was almost as good as if he really loved her. She had his loyalty, his promise that Ada would never endure the pain of knowing he sought pleasure in another. Could this not be enough for her to be happy?

Chapter 21
The Duke and Duchess

Kit found himself whistling as his valet dressed him for the evening. He had never whistled in his life, not even as a young boy. It was odd. There was a feeling of such contentment coursing through his veins. Happiness, he tasted the word on his tongue and found that it fit. He was amazingly, incandescently happy.

This morning he'd woken up to Ada in his arms, their legs tangled in the sheets and they'd made love again, slowly and half-asleep. It had been on the tip of his tongue to tell her how he truly felt. Lay it all at her mercy and hope the feelings were reciprocated. After last night, he was almost sure they were.

"I'd want you always, no matter the circumstances."

Those words tumbling from Ada's lips in the midst of passion had both soothed and inflamed his heart. He'd repeated them over and over in his mind. Ada wanted him, and not because of his position or status, but for who he was. Surely that was love. She'd left before he could voice his feelings, preoccupied with the preparations for the ball. He'd glimpsed her through a doorway checking flowers with the housekeeper, before scurrying off to something else, too busy even to join him for lunch. He smiled at her dedication. It seemed everything she did charmed him and the effort she put into their first ball as a couple seemed further evidence his feelings were returned.

He would tell her tonight. Take her aside to a balcony or one of the retiring rooms and confess his love. He allowed the fantasy to unspool in his mind, golden and tinged with delight. She would say she loved him too, just as much and as deeply, and then he would kiss her, gently at first but with a little more passion, until she pulled away with a laugh, reminding him that their guests were still in the ballroom.

"Your Grace, any preference for your cravat pin tonight?" asked his valet.

"The sapphire," he said. It reminded him of Ada's eyes.

He'd gone down early, hoping to catch a moment with his wife before the first guests trickled in, but it seemed the curiosity of a new Duchess had drawn a veritable crowd of the ton to arrive far sooner than was generally the custom.

He couldn't blame them for their fascination. Ada, clad in the finest silks tailored for the occasion and glittering in the Ducal jewels was like a shining star amongst them. She sparkled, drawing the eye of every person in the room. And Kit was no exception.

He did his part as host, circulating through the guests, offering polite greetings but his eyes went more often than not to his wife.

"You aren't being subtle at all," said Manderville, materialising at his side.

"I cannot be accused of anything untoward. She is my wife," replied Kit.

Manderville snorted. "I don't know that it's strictly polite to be undressing any woman with your eyes in public, even if she is yours by marriage."

Kit looked away from Ada with difficulty. "That wasn't what I was doing," he said far too quickly.

Manderville snorted again, then his expression turned serious. "You look happy Kit. I'm pleased for you. Your marriage doesn't appear to be the despondent affair you feared."

"No, indeed, I am happier than I ever thought I could be," he said.

A wide smile broke out on his friend's face making it clear why, despite Manderville's rakish ways, he was still much sought by the ladies. "I was worried about you. You seemed so certain she loved another when we last spoke. But look at you both. She turns to glance at you as many times as you do her. A love match after all."

Could it really be true? Kit had been convinced that Ada felt something akin to love for him already, but if Manderville saw it too then it wasn't just the manifestation of his own deepest desires.

"We have not spoken of it," he confessed. "I cannot be certain of her feelings."

"Then speak to her Kit. It is better to be certain of her affection than to live in this state of doubt. What is it that you fear?"

"That she feels nothing for me. That I hold no place in her heart," he confessed.

"I am certain that will not be the case. Speak with her and I am sure your happiness will be complete."

"You're right. Of course you are."

He straightened his waistcoat and adjusted his cuffs before glancing around the room for Ada. He caught sight of her and his face paled, heart sinking.

She wasn't alone.

Mellford was standing with her. Just a little closer than was strictly respectable. And from Ada's open smile, she had no issue with it. In fact, she appeared to be welcoming it wholeheartedly, laying her hand oh so delicately on his arm. Jealously, anger, and hurt flooded through Kit as the couple took to the floor for a dance.

He had agreed to take no other lovers. Ada had agreed no such thing. But to arrange her affair so flagrantly during the first ball of their marriage, that smarted of disrespect. She may love this Mellford, but she was still Kit's wife, still the Duchess of Aberlay and should conduct herself so.

"Kit, snap out of it," said Manderville.

"No, I don't think I will," he said through clenched teeth.

Manderville made to say something else, but Kit was already turning on his heel and striding out the ballroom. He was abruptly done with all of it. Who cared if it was his own party? Ada seemed to be happier with him out of the picture.

He found his way to his study and slumped in his favourite armchair, head in his hands. Doubt and fear clouded his mind. His wife, his beautiful Ada. Was she his? Or had he stolen her from another? The thought of her wanting another man was the cruellest of tortures.

There was a careful knock on his study. Kit lifted his head to see the subject of his agonised thoughts push open the door and step inside. He stared at her. God, she truly was the loveliest of creatures.

"You went missing. I came to find and bring you back," Ada said, a teasing lilt in her voice that even now had Kit responding.

He drowned his scotch in a single swig and set the glass down firmly on the table. "You seem to be managing fine without me," he said, "In fact it looks as though you already have my replacement lined up."

"I don't understand."

"Don't play the innocent. I saw you with Mellford. Saw the way you looked at him." He was standing too close to her in his rage. He could smell her delicate perfume, the soap on her skin.

"Mellford?" She had the nerve to sound confused. "How was I looking at him? What exactly do you think I've done?"

And what could Kit say to that? He was the one who'd dishonoured her, who'd forced their marriage, knowing he didn't have her heart. She had done nothing wrong. These were the natural consequences of his own actions. Abruptly the rage left him, leaving only despair.
"You will take him as your lover then. I will not impede you. Though I ask that you still fulfil your public duties to me as Duchess."

"What are you saying? What are you talking about? You think I want Mellford?"

"You were going to marry him! Of course, you want him. Instead, you're stuck with me and this marriage I forced you into."

Ada started laughing. The sound like a dagger to Kit's heart. Did she find his pain so amusing?

"Mellford proposed to me and I turned him down," she said.

"Because I dishonoured you."

"No my darling, I turned him down even before that because I was already hopelessly in love with you."

She cupped his face in her gloved hand and Kit found he couldn't speak.

"You, what, I," he tried but words deserted him completely.

She giggled. The most beautiful sound in the world. "Is it so shocking that I would fall in love with such a wonderful man. Though until now I thought he'd never return my feelings."

This was too much. That Ada could imagine for one possible second that she wasn't the object of his heart, the sole purpose of his misbegotten existence. He had to find the words to tell her.

"I love you," he managed to get out. "I think I've loved you from the first moment I laid eyes on you, certainly it didn't take much longer than that."

"Oh Kit, what fools we are. Driving ourselves mad with jealousy over other people when we've only ever loved each other."

Each word that came from her mouth was like water to a parched man, like a blessing from the heavens. He curled a hand around the nape of her neck possessively. "Only each other. No one else. You are my love Ada, my only love. I want no others and will have no others. For the rest of my life, only you."

She was crying now but from the smile on her face he could see it was from sheer, uncontrollable joy. "Yes, my love, no others. Not for me, and not for you," she agreed.

He kissed her then. How could he not. His dear beloved wife, who unbelievably loved him just as he loved her. Kit pressed her to him as tightly as he could, ravishing her with his mouth, with his tongue, eager to take possession of her body as he now knew he had complete possession of her heart. All doubt, all that wretched worry disappeared into undiluted happiness. Ada, his Ada. Everything was her.

Ada didn't think she'd ever been so happy in her life. And it was all due to Mellford! Kit had loved her all this time! Had loved her from the start. And here she'd been thinking she loved him alone, when in fact her love was returned. How much joy was it possible for one person to contain in their heart? Ada felt hers would burst from it. Kit was kissing her and she could feel now with every press of his lips just how much he did love her. She met his ardour with passion of her own, set alight now with the surety of knowing the one you loved was equally in love with you.

Kit's hands slid down, cupping her breast possessively. Ada arched into the touch with a groan. Through the layers of material, she could only just feel the heat of his hand, but it teased her with the thought of being skin to skin, of Kit's possessive touch on her naked body. What a wanton he was turning her into.

"Bedroom," he murmured.

"The guests," she protested weakly.

"We're newlyweds. Concessions must be made for that," he said.

She was sure it was frightfully rude for both hosts to leave in the middle of their own ball. But she allowed herself to be persuaded. The preparations she'd put so much effort into seemed a distant consideration when Kit was kissing her and touching her like this, his hands leaving a line of fire across her body.

She nodded her consent and he grinned, heaving her into his arms as if she weighed nothing.

"Kit!" she gasped, "You can't mean to carry me through the house like this!"

"Watch me," he said, not sounding even a bit out of breath as he all but raced up the stairs.

"God, what if one of the servants see us," she said, burying her face in his neck.

"Then they'll laugh at me in my haste. No one will think anything ill of you Ada."

"But I feel as much haste as you," she whispered into his ear.

Kit almost missed a step. "God darling, save it for when we are between the sheets. I fear if you make *all* my blood rush south, my body won't work well enough to get to our destination."

It seemed forever before Kit was carrying her through the ducal chambers, slamming the door behind him and laying Ada across their massive bed before clambering over her, his body a hard line across hers.

"My darling," he said, cupping her face before pressing his lips to hers. Ada moaned, sliding a hand down to remove Kit's jacket and tugging his shirt from his breeches, eager to get her hands on his skin.

"That's it my love. Touch me. Wherever you want. I am yours," he murmured before ducking down to kiss her more intently than before, his tongue slipping into her mouth.

With Kit's help she divested him of his clothing until his naked body lay across the sheets and there was nothing hiding him from Ada's covetous gaze. She took the time to eye him appreciatively and he allowed it, a self-satisfied smile playing across his lips.

"Are you pleased with your husband, my love?"

"Very pleased," she said. "I'd be more pleased if he'd make love to me."

"Isn't that what we've been doing?"

"I admit I am inexperienced, but last time we did this, I distinctly remember having less clothes on," she said gesturing to her full ballgown, rumpled but otherwise intact.

Kit laughed. "My darling, that is easily remedied. You already know of my skill in removing your clothes."

"I suggest you put it to good use then," she ordered.

"My Duchess," he said, deft fingers unlacing the ties of Ada's clothes, "I am forever at your service."

Every inch of skin he uncovered, he pressed soft kisses to. Ada felt her whole body melt under his ministrations. Kit's dark head moving slowly lower. The underside of her breast, her naval, and finally he pressed his lips to her inner thigh. Ada let out a murmur of pleasure, winding her fingers in his hair and allowing her legs to fall apart.

He wasted no time in licking into her core. "You taste divine my love," he groaned, before burying his face enthusiastically between her thighs. Ada cried out as his tongue circled her nub, tilting her hips up into Kit's face. Clever fingers found her entrance and thrust in, once, twice and then Ada was peaking, Kit's tongue and fingers playing her to perfection. Her entire body shuddered, legs trembling around him as that familiar pleasure rocked through her.

"Sweetheart, I need to be inside you," she heard as she came to. Her husband was holding himself carefully above her. From the tense clench of his jaw and his dark eyes it was clear how much he wanted her. Reaching down, Ada grasped his hot length and guided it inside.

They moaned in unison. That first delicious drag of Kit inside her inflaming every part of her body. The feeling of being joined with him, knowing he loved her, it was the most exquisite pleasure Ada had ever felt in her life. She clung to him, moaning as he began to rock their hips together, her legs lifting to wrap around him.

"Ada," he groaned, burying his face in her neck.

She touched him greedily, covetously. Her husband, her love. He was hers. Her hands ran over the strong muscles of his back, up to his neck, before digging her fingers firmly into the thick locks she loved so much. All the while his hips rolled into her, creating a rhythm that left her teetering on the edge once more.

"Kit, God, please," she was barely coherent.

His hand slid down to her folds and found her nub, tracing quick, tight circles there. He knew exactly how to touch her. Ada cried out and shuddered, clenching around him, her fingers claws against his scalp as her spine arched off the bed. Wave after wave of pleasure careened through her as Kit remade her into something that was solely his.

Her husband cried out hoarsely. His thrusts hitting harder. A wet heat flooded inside her as he gave one last stuttering thrust, burying himself deep, his entire length trembling against hers. He was so beautiful thought Ada as she stared at her husband's face, his features contorted with pleasure. All of his tightly wound control lost as he reached ecstasy in her body.

It seemed impossible that such a man could love her, but when his eyes opened and he looked at her, his gaze was filled with so much affection that Ada knew at last that he truly did.

"My love," he murmured, ducking down for a kiss, getting more of her chin than her actual mouth.

She giggled. "Your aim is slightly off."

He grinned. "Making love to you would make any man loopy. Let me try again."

This time, his lips found hers. A searing kiss that laid bare all the passion and love he felt for her. Ada returned it wholeheartedly.

THE END

Also by the Author

The Highland Beast

A name that spreads fear

Even Rosamund Macfie has heard stories about The Highland Beast, though she lives in the Scottish Lowlands. Rumours of his horrific appearance and terrifying exploits are used to scare children into obedience. However, she never thought she would meet him, let alone find herself bound to be his bride.

A marriage she cannot escape

Now the fate of her clan rests on her wedding Lachlan Rodrhu, or as he is better known, The Highland Beast. Rosamund is terrified of the future that awaits her as the wife of such a man, but circumstance offers her no other choice. With a heavy heart and dread in her bones, Rosamund says the words that will tie her to The Highland Beast forever.

A man bound by duty

More monster than man, Lachlan Rodrhu, laird of clan Rodrhu, is well aware that he would make a bad husband for any woman, and he has no intention of burdening himself with a wife that would fear and hate him. But the death of his brother and heir changes everything. Suddenly Lachlan must marry and produce an heir and it must be done quickly. An old betrothal contract between the Rodrhus and Macfies makes Rosamund Macfie the most convenient solution to Lachlan's problem, even if it means resigning himself to a cold and unhappy marriage. Because if anything is certain, it is that no woman could ever love The Highland Beast.

Printed in Great Britain
by Amazon